Love
AT THE
LAKE

D1371990

THERESA BERWEILER

PAGE PUBLISHING, INC.
Conneaut Lake, PA

First originally published by Page Publishing 2019

ISBN 978-1-64544-351-3 (pbk)
ISBN 978-1-64544-352-0 (digital)

Printed in the United States of America

For Dennis and Joshua, my light and my heart

For all the women in my life who supported me during the writing of this book: My sisters: Tina, Loretta, Kathleen, the 604 girls, Marianne, Ginny, Judy and my scrapin' girls.

Don't think about the things you can't do.
If you can dream it, you can do it.

PROLOGUE

*K*elsey felt a contraction, and tears sprang to her eyes. Why were they putting her through the whole birth process? The doctors knew the baby was dead! Why couldn't they just do a C-section? Why does she have to go through the pain of giving birth to a dead baby? She had been waiting eight months for this child, and in the end, she wasn't even going to have him or her! She was only nineteen years old, for God's sake! How was this even happening? And where was Gene? He promised to be here when the baby was born. Out on the road…again! The band that had started in her father's garage was starting to become successful and that meant touring. At least that was what the record company said.

"Here comes another one!" the nurse said, looking at the monitor. "Time to push."

"I can't!" she cried out, "Gene's not here yet. He promised to be *here!* I need him here!" Kelsey dissolved into tears.

"Come on, baby," her mom said, "you can do this."

"No, Mom!" Kelsey cried. "I need Gene, please!" Kelsey gripped the sides of the bed as the contraction got stronger.

"I'm sorry, Kelsey, but we can't wait any longer." The doctor moved into position. "Okay, get ready, *push!*"

December 1973
Seven months earlier

They had just pulled up to their spot at the lake and Gene jumped out of the car.

"C'mon, Kels, I want to show you something!"

What's wrong with him? Kelsey thought. It's the middle of December, the lake is frozen, and it's freezing out there. What could he possibly have to show her?

"I'm coming!" Kelsey yelled back. She caught up with him at the logs they had usually met at before they both got their driver's licenses. "What's so important?" she asked breathlessly, "I'm freezing!" She huddled against him to keep warm.

"This," Gene said, opening a small box that held her engagement ring.

"Oh, Gene!" Kelsey was speechless.

Gene got down on one knee, held out the ring, and said, "I love only you, Kelsey. Will you marry me?"

"Yes! Yes!" she cried as he slipped the ring on her finger.

"I couldn't do it anywhere but here," Gene said, hugging her. "I wanted to wait until spring. But the band is leaving soon for a tour, and I was hoping you'd go with me?"

"That would be so much fun! We'll have to ask my parents." she replied. She was on semester break from her freshman year at Colorado Mesa University. She could go out with them for a few weeks.

"They're cool. They'll let you go." Gene said. "Let's go back to the car. It's freezing!"

"Really?" she laughed.

They ran back to the car, turned the heat on, and started making out, celebrating their engagement. They moved to the back seat and started undressing each other.

"Gene, I don't have one with me," she whispered, reaching into the front pocket of his pants, "Do you?"

"No, I don't" he groaned. "I changed my pants after rehearsal and left my wallet at home."

They looked at each other with longing. "It couldn't happen just one time, right?" Gene asked, pushing her hair behind her ear and kissing her neck.

Kelsey groaned and whispered, "Maybe not."

He kissed her again. "Take a chance?" he asked, caressing her breasts.

"Wouldn't be the worst thing if it did happen," she answered breathlessly, losing all self-control. "We are getting married." Gene nodded. They smiled at each other and took a chance.

When they got home later that night Kelsey and Gene told both sets of parents about the engagement. Neither was happy about it. They both agreed the kids were too young. But they pretended to accept it so they wouldn't run away and elope. At least this way they could control them a little. Maybe persuade them to wait until Kelsey finished school. Then Kelsey missed her period.

* * *

Kelsey

She sat on the exam table at her gynecologist office. She knew what the test results would be. She was sure she was pregnant. The thing is, she wasn't upset. She was happy! She and Gene had talked all the time about all the kids they would have, taking them out on tour, schooling them in life and not a classroom. Of course, she had planned on getting her teaching certification first, but they could work around that. This baby was going to be their ticket to freedom! She couldn't wait to tell him! They could get married right away! Get an apartment! Her parents, on the other hand, would hit the ceiling! So would Gene's.

"Mrs. Kelly, Kelsey," Dr. Kavanaugh said as he entered the room. He looked down at his folder and then at Kelsey and smiled. "Well, congratulations, young lady, you're going to be a mother!" Kelsey smiled and turned toward her mother who had gone pale.

"How far along is she?" her mother asked.

"About six weeks," he replied. "Now here's a schedule of when we need to see you," he said, handing her some papers. "And the second page is about diet and exercise. You should give birth around the second week in September. Go see the receptionist about your appointments, and here's a prescription for some prenatal vitamins."

"Mom! You're going to be a grandmother again!" Kelsey said, excitedly. Her older brother Jerry already had two kids. Her mother smiled at her weakly.

"Thank you, Ron," she said to Dr. Kavanaugh.

"Mom, are you all right?" Kelsey asked later, in the car. "You're very pale."

"Just trying to absorb the news." Her mom pulled into a department store parking lot and turned off the engine. She turned toward Kelsey. "How did this happen, Kelsey? We talked about birth control, and you told me you and Gene were using condoms."

"We did, Mom," Kelsey said. "Every time. Well, except that one time last month when Gene proposed." Kelsey looked lovingly at her engagement ring. "We thought it would be okay." Kelsey smiled at the memory.

"You're actually happy about this, aren't you?" her mother asked, appalled. "You realize your life is over, don't you? Forget about going back to school!"

"Mom, calm down," Kelsey answered. "Gene and I have been talking about getting married and having lots of kids for years now. Why are you so upset?"

"Because you're only nineteen, honey!" her mother cried. "How am I going to tell your father? He doesn't even know you're having sex!" Her mother laid her head on the steering wheel.

"You were twenty when you had Jerry," Kelsey reminded her. "Was your life over?"

"That was different," she said. "I was married, and I did what was expected of me." Her mother became very agitated. "Kelsey, you're so young! You have such a bright future ahead of you. You want to be a music teacher at our school. You want to help kids with special needs, remember?"

"That's what you always told me I wanted." Kelsey said, looking at her, pointedly.

"What?" her mother asked, a little shocked. "It's not what you want?"

"It's not the only thing I want, Mom!" Kelsey cried. "Yes, I want to teach music at the school, but I also want to marry Gene, go on the road with the band, have kids, live life!"

Her mother looked at her and shook her head.

Later that same day

"Gene!" Kelsey shouted. She had left a message with Danny to tell Gene to meet her at the lake. Gene was waiting for her at their spot. His face lit up whenever he saw her and his heart always did a little flip.

"What did the doctor say?" he asked. Kelsey had told him she suspected she might be pregnant. She smiled at him and nodded her head.

Gene picked her up and swung her around. "Woo-hoo!" he cried. "They can't stop us now! Let's get married tomorrow!"

Kelsey laughed and nodded in agreement. She couldn't wait for their future.

CHAPTER ONE

August 2010

"FyreByrds, FyreByrds!" The crowd shouted, chanting their name over and over, willing them to come out onto the stage to start the show. These guys have been at it for over thirty-five years and still as popular today as ever.

* * *

Kelsey

She sat among the fans, wondering what is she doing here? Would he remember her? Would he recognize Emily? Guess who she really is? She didn't know, but she had to find out. They both needed to know, and Gene deserved the truth.

* * *

Gene

He pulled back the curtain a little. He likes to get a look at the crowd before each show. Let's be honest, he's scoping out the women to find one to go back to his hotel room with him. He's been doing this ever since he broke up with Tracey five years ago. He hates going back to his hotel alone after a show. There are a few lookers at the tables down front. God, they all look so young! Maybe he should go for their mothers! Ha! That blond to the right of the stage looks strangely familiar. He allows his eyes to scan the whole room. Nice-looking crowd. Wait…his heart did a little flip. Who is that at the bar? She looks like…no, can't be! He hasn't thought about *her* for years. It hurts too much. He tries to get another look.

"Hey, Gene!" called the drummer. "Time for a huddle." He looked back at the bar. Someone was blocking her. He drops the curtain. Showtime.

"Ladies and gentlemen! Please make welcome… The FyreByrds!" The band takes the stage and starts the first song.

The crowd is going wild! The concert is going well. Everyone is having a good time. About thirty minutes into the show, Gene spotted that blond again down front. He gets a better look at her. Wow, she looked really familiar. He decided to talk to her.

"Hey, sweetheart! How are you tonight?" he said to her into the mike. She smiles at him. Her eyes look just like his mother's! "You look really familiar… Have we ever slept together?" he said flippantly. The rest of the band laughs.

"No!" she yelled out, blushing. "But you know my mother."

Holy shit! "I slept with your mother? Hell, I'm getting old" Gene joked. "Is she here? I'd love to see her again and say hello." Please don't be here, he thought. The guys laughed and slapped each other on the back like boys do.

"Yes, she's here. She's sitting at the bar," said the blond. Gene freezes and thought oh shit! The rest of the band laughed again.

"You naughty boy!" says Kevin, who played fiddle and banjo.

"Ooh." The crowd laughed.

Uh-oh. He hopes she's not a dog! He hopes he remembers her! Gene looks toward the front of the club where the bar is located. "Hey, Marty," he said to the lighting director, "shine a light on the bar." The crowd oohed and aahed in anticipation.

The spotlight slowly scans the bar. *There she is.* The woman he has not thought about in over thirty years yet has been a part of every song he's ever written.

"Right there, Marty!" The light stops. He can't believe it! It's her! Kelsey! His face goes pale. "My God," he said, softly to himself.

The band looks at each other. Gene looks like he's seen a ghost! He locks eyes with her, and in that instant, he knows everything. He can't move. His heart started palpitating. He jumps from the stage and runs toward her. The crowd parts for him, like in a movie. Gene stops right in front of her. She's still so beautiful.

"You're here." He panted. "I can't believe you're here." He reached out and enveloped her in a big hug. He can't let go. She hugged him back. "She's my daughter," he whispered in her ear. It's not a question. It's the truth.

Kelsey whispered back, "Yes."

He broke the hug to look at her. They both have tears in their eyes.

* * *

Emily

She watched Gene's face when he saw her mother. Wow, he looked like he's seen a ghost! She turned and looked at her mother's face. Her mother looked at Gene and smiled. Gene ran toward Kelsey and they hugged. Oh my god! They still love each other!

* * *

Danny

He wasn't really paying attention to what Gene was saying as he tuned his guitar. Gene had slept with so many women over the years. The conversation with the girl tonight was no different than any other night. He glances at the bar when Gene told Marty to stop the spotlight. Holy shit! It's Kelsey. The one girl he couldn't forget! Pills and booze had helped dull the pain over the years. What the hell is she doing here? Crap! He was going to need a bottle of tequila as well as the pills tonight!

After the show, Gene and the rest of the band go out to sign autographs. They've always done this, after every show. He knows he would not have any success in this business if not for the fans. He sees Kelsey in the distance with their daughter. He had whispered to Kelsey to wait for him after the show. After the crowd left Gene approaches both of them. Before he can say anything, the rest of the band descends on them.

"Hey, Kelsey!"

"Long time!"

"How've you been?"

"Who's this beauty with you?" The guys are really excited to see her. She was there in the beginning with them.

Gene tried to catch Kelsey's eye. He finally did. He jerked his head to the left. He moved to the left, so did she. Emily watched them as they move away from the rest of the band. They sat down on a couple of stools by the bar.

They just sat and looked at each other. Gene wanted to reach out and touch her but he's afraid she'll disappear. The bartender brings them each a shot of Jack.

"I thought we could use this" Kelsey said. They knocked them back and she began to talk.

"Pete passed about five years ago," she began. "Emily and he were very close. She has always been curious about his side of the family. You remember, he hadn't spoken to his parents in years. As a family, we were never close to them and he didn't like to talk about them." Kelsey took a deep breath. "She took a DNA test on Ancestry. com to see if she could find some of Pete's relatives. It came back that…that…she could not be Pete's daughter." Kelsey gulped back a sob. Gene just sat there, stunned, trying to absorb the news.

Kelsey puts her hand over his on the bar. "Gene, I am so sorry! I swear, I thought she was Pete's. If I had known, I would have told you! I would never have kept her from you!"

Gene felt a familiar tingle when Kelsey touched his hand. He remembers exactly when it happened. The last time they were together. The benefit concert for her parents' school, the Woodhaven School for Special Needs Children. June of 1980. He and the band used to do it every year if they were in the area. At that show, they hadn't seen each other for about six years. After she suffered a still-birth and lost their baby, James, when she was nineteen. During the show they realized they still loved each other. They had one magical night together. She had had a fight earlier that week with her boy-friend, Pete McCoury. But afterward, Gene just left. He still couldn't give her what she wanted…a home, family, stability. He needed to be on the road, playing music.

"Was he a good father?" Gene asked quietly. He had to know.

"Yes, to Emily and our son, PJ." Kelsey replied. "He was a great father."

Gene looks back at Emily, talking with the rest of the band. There's no doubt she's his. "She looks just like my mother." He said to Kelsey. Wow, a daughter, he thought. He has a son, Declan with his ex.

"Oh my god! She does!" Kelsey exclaimed. "How did I not see it?"

"Can I meet her?" He asked, looking back at Kelsey. "Of course," Kelsey said, squeezing his hand. "Hey Em, c'mere."

Emily walked over, shyly, and stood in front of him. They just looked at each other.

Before Kelsey could say anything, Gene extended his hand and said "Hi, I'm Gene. I'm your father."

Emily smiled back and said, "Hi. I'm Emily. I'm your daughter."

They both laughed as they embraced.

CHAPTER TWO

* * *

Emily

Wow, she was actually meeting her biological father. Gene Miller of the Fyrebyrds. A bonafide country-rock superstar. Her dad, Pete McCoury, was the greatest person she had ever known, and initially, she felt very disloyal to him when her mother suggested they go to a Fyrebyrds concert and meet Gene after they got the test results. They talked about it for months. Mom was so upset! She really had no idea that her dad wasn't her biological father. Mom still hasn't told her the details of their relationship. She tried asking her many aunts and uncles. (Mom has four brothers and three sisters.) But they were very closed mouth about it. They said, "Your mother will tell you when she's ready." Even her grandmother was mum on the subject. Her grandfather was in the early stages of Alzheimer's.

Emily and Gene went to an all-night diner and talked the rest of the night. He asked her a lot of questions about her childhood and her relationship with her dad. He also told her about the night she was conceived and why he left. Emily told him her parents were married a few months later.

"Has your mother ever talked about me? We've known each other since we were kids, you know." Gene said.

"Really? No, she's never said a word! My whole family is very quiet on the subject of you." said Emily. Gene was not surprised. "Please tell me," she said.

"Well," Gene said. "It was 1963. I was ten and your mother was eight. My family had just moved in across the street from your grandparents' house. My mother and I walked over in hope that there were some kids my age to play with. We hit the jackpot with your mother's family. Your mom answered the door. 'Is your mother home, dear?' my mother said. Your grandmother came to the door and invited us in. I met your aunts and uncles. In fact, your uncles became my best friends and your Uncle Jerry taught me how to play guitar. But your mother...she kept staring at me." Gene shook his head, smiling at the memory. 'What are looking at.' I asked. 'We are going to get married someday.' she answered." Gene stopped talking and laughed. "I told her that there was no way we were getting married because girls were gross!" He laughed again. "My mother slapped me on the back of the head and told me to apologize. We started dating in high school. The rest is history."

"The history is what I'm curious about," Emily said, smiling coyly.

"That, you'll have to talk to your mother about," Gene said, not taking the bait.

By this time, it was almost 6:00 AM. "Wow, it's late or rather early! Mom and I have to leave for home in a few hours. I have a class this afternoon and have to work tonight." She was studying for her master's in nursing and had a shift in the NICU later that night.

"I wish you could stay longer. We have another show here tonight. I haven't even had a chance to talk to Kelsey," said Gene wistfully.

Emily had seen the way they looked at each other. There hasn't been another man in my mother's life since Dad died. Mischievously, Emily said "Mom could stay. She doesn't have anything to get back to." Gene looked at her hopefully. "I'll make it happen." He smiled, glad she was on his side.

Kelsey was awakened by someone coming into the hotel room. It's Emily. She glances at the clock. It's almost 7:00 AM. Gene and

Emily had been talking all night! From the look on Emily's face, it went well.

"Morning, Mom," Emily said, lying down on the bed.

"Morning, honey. How did it go?" she asked as she got out of bed. They were driving home in a few hours.

"Really well. Gene's a great guy. We're going to make plans to get together when he gets back home. Did you know he lives only about two hours from us?" Emily paused. "He was hoping to talk to you before we leave."

Oh no, Kelsey is not ready for that! "We can't. You have to get back for your class." There, problem solved.

"I have to get back, but you don't," Emily said. What was Emily talking about! Of course, she had to get back! She has things to do! Didn't she?

"You have no committee meetings, no garden club, and school doesn't start for another three weeks." Emily said. Kelsey taught music at her parents' school. Emily took her mother's hand in hers. "I think you need to talk to him, Mom. You both need some closure on this." Kelsey looked at Emily. "Gene wants you to call his room in a few hours. Here's his number. He's going to get some sleep. They have another show here tonight."

She stared at the piece of paper. Talk to Gene? Kelsey hadn't thought she would have to talk to Gene again. She's not sure she's forgiven him for...well...she doesn't want to think about that now. Emily is right about one thing. There is absolutely nothing in Colorado that she has to get back to. Lord, please get me through this!

"How are you going to get home?" she asked.

"I'll take the train," she answered.

* * *

Emily

She was on the train a few hours later. Her mom had looked very nervous when she gave her Gene's cell number. She really hopes she calls him. She knows she did the right thing. She could see that those two belonged together. Dear Jesus, please let this happen. Mom deserves to be happy. Amen.

CHAPTER THREE

*G*ene was eating a late lunch when his cell phone rang. Emily had texted him that she had given her mother his number. He had been staring at the phone all afternoon waiting for it to ring. He grabbed it and answered before the second ring.

"Hello?" he said.

"Hi, it's me, Kelsey," she said, haltingly.

"Hi," he said again. There was an awkward silence.

"Am I interrupting something? I'm interrupting. I can call back, let me call you back, you're probably busy." she sputtered.

"No!" he yelled. "Don't hang up! Please! I need to see you. Please come to the show tonight, and we'll go out after and talk." He paused, waiting for her answer.

"I can't," she said, laughing nervously. "I don't have a ticket."

"Don't worry," he said, laughing too, "you know the lead singer." They both laughed.

* * *

Kelsey

What the hell was she doing? Front row at the concert with a backstage pass. The band always bought out the first row at shows and brought down people from the nosebleed section to sit there. She was sitting with true-blue FyreByrd fans! But Emily was right, she and Gene had to talk about this. Hopefully, the Lord would give her the right words.

Last night, when the rest of the guys in the band saw Kelsey they were all over her with hugs and questions. They hadn't seen each other since the beginning in her father's garage, back in the seventies. Danny was a little quiet. He kept looking at Kelsey and then looking away. They had a little history after she and Gene broke up. After about thirty minutes and a few drinks, he loosened up and started smiling at her. They jammed, sang, and talked far into the night, almost as long as Gene and Emily. They even wanted Kelsey to sing with them onstage tomorrow night! Fat chance! The fans were here to see the Fyrebyrds, not some middle aged music teacher. Besides, she had to prepare herself for her talk with Gene, afterward.

During the show Gene never took his eyes off her. Every song was for her tonight. Kelsey never took her eyes off him either. This was the man she had fallen in love when they were both teenagers.

"You know, folks, there's an old friend of ours here tonight," he said about halfway through the show, "She was there in the beginning when we were just a band in her dad's garage. Her brothers were original members. She was our only 'girl singer.' With your permission, I'd like to bring her up to do a song with us. Please make welcome, Kelsey McCoury!"

The crowd cheered and clapped. Kelsey sat frozen in her chair looking at him, shaking her head and mouthing, "No way!"

* * *

Kelsey

Was he kidding? Get onstage with them? Yeah, she had jammed with the band last night, but that was just fooling around. The security guard came over, smiling and offered her his arm. "I've been instructed not to take 'no' for an answer," he said. The rest of the guys were smiling and motioning for her to come up on the stage. The crowd cheered. How could she refuse?

Kelsey walked up on the stage. "What are you doing?" she said to Gene, "I can't sing with you guys!"

"Sure, you can," he said, pushing her toward the mic. "Just like old times. Riding a bike."

"C'mon, Kels," Danny said, "you can do it."

Kevin smiled at her, handed her his fiddle, and said, "You got this. We'll do 'He Darked the Sun' Linda's version."

She tuned up the fiddle and looked at Stucky and Cap. They nodded and smiled their approval. Here goes nothing! Gene counted off, "1, 2, 3, 4, 1!"

"And with the length of his mind, he darked the sun…" As they sang together, she felt the jolt of him in a place that she hadn't felt in quite a while. She could feel his excitement, too, as he sang to her.

Chapter Four

*A*fter the concert, Gene took her to the same diner he had taken Emily. The waitress was an old friend and would make sure no one bothered them. There would be a certain amount of privacy. After they ordered, he just stared at her. He still couldn't believe she was here! She hadn't changed a bit. God, she was still so beautiful.

"You still got it," Gene said, meaning musically, "you did a great job on that song. The fans loved it. They were asking about you at the meet and greet after the show."

"Well, that's nice of them. I'm just glad you picked a song that I knew! You weren't always that considerate! In fact, if I remember correctly, you enjoyed playing tricks and embarrassing me when we were kids!" she said. "Remember my eighth grade Spring Concert?"

He smiled. He remembered. "But you could always handle yourself."

"Didn't really have a choice!" She laughed.

He paused. "May I ask you about your life?" he said as their food arrived.

* * *

Kelsey

She smiled back. He was still the best-looking man she had ever seen! Wavy brown, rock star hair, and hazel eyes. She answered all his questions. She had had the life she had always wanted—husband, kids, house with the white picket fence, rewarding career, the

American Dream. She and Pete moved to California after they got married and she taught out there for about three years. When she got pregnant with PJ, she knew she wanted him and Emily to grow up in the mountains of Colorado around her family. So, they moved back, and she started teaching at her parents' school for kids with special needs. Pete had gotten a job with her father's engineering firm. It had been a good life.

"What about you," she asked. "Marriage, kids?"

Gene's face grew a little sad. "Yeah, I did the marriage thing. A few years after I last saw you. It didn't last. I was on the road all the time. The best thing about those years, though, is my son, Declan." His face changed to a look of pride. "Dec is a musician like his old man, married with a three-year-old daughter and an eight-month-old son. Sophie and Dylan." Like any proud grandpa, he took out his wallet to show her pictures.

"You're a grandfather! Wow!" she said. "Oh, Gene! They're beautiful!"

"Umm, what about Tracy?" Kelsey asked. She had read about their relationship in the tabloids. Tracy was a very talented song-writer and quite a few years younger than Gene.

"That didn't last," Gene said, shaking his head. "I told Tracy in the beginning that I was not interested in any more children. She accepted that for the first few years. Then she started talking about her biological clock, about how cute babies were, about us getting married, blah, blah, blah. I wasn't budging. After five years, she finally left me for someone closer to her own age, and last I heard, she was pregnant with her second baby." He said, shrugging.

"Any regrets?" she asked.

"No, not really," he answered. "How 'bout you? Any regrets?"

"Maybe just one," she said, looking down at her empty plate. He looked sad again, knowing what she was thinking.

"Do you ever visit him?" she asked quietly.

"I usually make it on his birthday," he said, looking down.

"Funny," she said. "That's the only day I *can't* go to the cemetery. No wonder I never saw you there." They both sighed.

"Hey," he said suddenly, to break the mood, "let's go get a drink. We could both use one."

"Sounds good," she said, relieved.

They went to the hotel bar where the band was staying. Kelsey was not able to get another room for the extra night, so Gene gave Kelsey his room and moved his things to Kevin's room. They ordered drinks and continued talking. While Kelsey went to the ladies room, Gene spotted a jukebox in the corner. He went to have a look. Wow, there were so many songs from their growing up years, the years when they were falling in love. Gene started feeding quarters into the machine and picking songs.

"Hey," he said when she returned, "see if you remember these songs." They started dancing and reminiscing with each song. Finally, after an hour or so and a few more drinks "their" song started playing. "Crazy" by Patsy Cline. Gene held Kelsey close as they danced.

* * *

Gene

What a great night! He didn't want it to end. Holding her, talking, catching up on each other's lives. He was falling in love with her all over again. There's "their" song! Wow, he really wants to kiss her.

* * *

Kelsey

She can't believe this night. How could she be falling in love again after all these years. Oh my god! "Their" song! She looks into his eyes. She really wants him to kiss her. Finally, he does. It was slow, soft, and sweet. They continued to dance and kiss. When the song ended, she took his hand and they walked to the elevator. The bartender, who had been watching them for the last half hour, yelled out "'Bout time!" as they passed the bar. They both laughed at him, blushing. She pushed the button for the sixth floor where her room was.

Gene and Kelsey couldn't keep their hands off each other. As they made out in the elevator, he pressed her against the wall. She gasped when she felt his erection against her and then groaned with desire. They continued to make out while walking to her room.

"Where's your key?" he asked between kisses.

"In my back pocket," she answered breathlessly. He reached in and pulled it out. They stumbled into the room and quickly started undressing each other.

When Kelsey pulled off Gene's pants, she dug her hand into the front pocket.

"If I remember correctly…" She pulled out a condom. "Ta-da!" They both smiled. He had always kept them in his front pocket in case his wallet got stolen. He had his priorities straight. Some things never change! They smiled at each other as they both fell on the bed.

Afterward, they held each other the way they used to, like spoons in a drawer. "We still fit," Gene said and kissed her shoulder. Just then her phone pinged.

"Who could that be?" Kelsey said, reaching for her purse on the night stand.

"Don't answer it," Gene said, pulling her back toward him.

"I have to," she said, grabbing her phone. "It's four in the morning. It could be an emergency." She read the text, started laughing, and couldn't stop.

"What's so funny?" he asked.

"Your daughter!" Kelsey laughed. Gene smiled. He liked the sound of that.

"Dear, Mom," Kelsey read, "I hope you are having a great night. I want you to be safe. I put two condoms in your purse." Kelsey started laughing again, reaching for her purse. Gene started blushing.

"Two? Who does she think I am?" he said, shaking his head. Despite what he said, they made use of both of them.

CHAPTER FIVE

* * *

Gene

*H*e opened his eyes, a few hours later, a little disoriented at first. He rolled over, saw her sleeping next to him, and smiled, remembering last night. He got up to go to the bathroom and brush his teeth. The only thing he loved more than sex after a show was sex the next morning. He checked his wallet. He always kept a spare there! He got back into bed and "spooned" her, waking her gently.

"Hey, good morning." Gene said slipping his hand around her waist and kissing her shoulder. He started fondling her breasts. Kelsey stirred and rolled over to face him.

"Good morning," she said, smiling.

He kissed her deeply. "Hey, you brushed too!" he said.

"Of course! I remember what you like to do in the morning!" she said. They made very good use of the last condom.

When they were spent, Gene looked at Kelsey and said, "We have to talk." Kelsey looked at him questioningly.

"I don't want this to be a onetime thing." He continued earnestly, "I want to see you again. I want to take you out on dates. I want to get to know you and fall in love with you again. I want us to finally have the relationship we missed out on." He looked at her to see what her reaction would be.

"So do I," Kelsey said, relieved. She had been trying to think of a way to say the same words to him. Would it work this time? Could she forgive everything that had happened?

A few hours later, they were packed and ready to go. They were driving to Kelsey's house to spend a few days and plan out how they were going to see each other. Last night's show was the last one for a few weeks. The rest of the band was taking the tour bus to their homes. They would get together for a rehearsal in a few weeks. Emily was going to come by later for dinner. PJ was practically living with his girlfriend, Meghan, so they could count on some privacy.

They arrived at Kelsey's house just before Emily. They decided to order Chinese for dinner. It was Em's favorite. Kelsey tried PJ a few times on his phone, but it went to voice mail. PJ was not happy about the whole situation of Pete not being Emily's biological father. PJ idolized his dad and took his death very hard. Wait until he found out Kelsey and Gene were going to be dating! He would not be happy at all! PJ had squashed several attempts by Kelsey to start dating over the last five years. Kelsey hadn't been emotionally strong enough before to stand up for herself. But Gene was different. Pete's last words to her was, "It's your turn to be happy." And that's what she intended to be. How PJ handles it is up to him.

It was a great evening. Emily and Gene looked at all the old pictures from her childhood and she told him all the stories behind them. They were really getting to know each other. Kelsey dug out her old scrapbooks so Gene could tell Emily about their years together. After she left, Kelsey and Gene lay on her bed watching TV, talking and holding hands.

* * *

Kelsey

Something was tickling her neck. She slowly came out of the sleep she was in and realized that it was Gene kissing her neck. Wow, this man had some appetite! Not that she was complaining! After they finished, Gene said he was hungry. "Help yourself to anything in the fridge. Bring me back something too."

* * *

Gene

It had only been a few days, and already she was ordering him around! Bring her something back? Of course, he would. He got out of bed and headed toward the kitchen. As he opened the door to the frig and stared at the contents trying to decide what they wanted to eat, he heard a young man's voice, "Who the hell are you and what are you doing in my kitchen?"

Gene looked up and saw a younger version of Pete McCoury staring at him, angrier than wet hen. It triggered a memory. He had gone to Pete's place after that last argument with Kelsey, the night Emily had been conceived. Same old thing, she wanted a home and a family, he wanted the road.

When Pete answered the door, he had sneered, "What do you want?"

"Do you love her?" Gene asked.

"More than anything," Pete answered.

"Then take care of her," he told him. Pete's expression softened and he nodded. Gene left and never looked back.

"Hi," Gene said, coming back to the present, closing the refrigerator door and extending his hand, "you must be PJ. I'm Gene."

PJ ignored Gen's hand and yelled, "I don't care who you are, you need to leave my house right now!"

* * *

Kelsey

She smiled as she heard Gene get out of bed to go get them something to eat, grumbling about her ordering him around. It was going be nice having a man around to wait on her occasionally. He was so easy too. Maybe she'd reserve her judgment until she sees what he brings back! She heard the front door open and PJ's voice, yelling. Uh-oh! She leaped out of bed, threw on her robe, and ran toward the kitchen.

"You need to leave my house right now!" PJ was yelling.

"Peter Jacob McCoury! Where are your manners?" Kelsey admonished him. "Did you leave them at Meghan's? How dare you speak to a guest in our home that way!"

PJ looked at the way his mother was dressed, or not dressed, threw a disgusted look at Gene, and stomped off to his room. "PJ, get back here right now and apologize!" she yelled after him.

"Let him go," Gene said. "He's upset. This was not the best way to meet your mom's new boyfriend."

"He's never had to before," she said, looking down the hall after him then looking at Gene. "You're the first man I've dated since his father died."

"Really? Wow, then this is really tough for him," Gene said. "Let him calm down, and we'll talk in the morning. C'mon, let's go to bed." He put his arm around her and steered her back to the bedroom.

"Boyfriend, huh?" she said, smiling at him, cocking her head.

"Yeah," Gene said, smiling back and cocking his head too. "First since Pete, huh?"

"Yeah," Kelsey said, putting her head on his shoulder. Gene hugged her and kissed her head.

In the morning, PJ was gone. He texted Kelsey that he would be back after Gene had left.

CHAPTER SIX

From the doorway of the kitchen, Gene watched Kelsey's face tear up as she looked at her phone. This was not good.

"Hey, darling," he said as he walked into the kitchen and gave her a hug. "What's for breakfast? I could eat a horse!" He hoped that would distract her. She quickly wiped her eyes.

"What would you like?" she asked brightly. "I can make just about anything you want." She smiled, pretending everything was all right. They settled on blueberry pancakes, bacon, coffee, and tea (for Kelsey). While she was cooking, he sneaked a peek at her phone and read PJ's text. Damn that boy! How could he hurt his mother like that? Could Gene fix this? He wanted her to be happy. *Should* he fix this?

"What do you want to do today? I am totally free," he said as he devoured pancakes and bacon.

"What do you usually do after a run of shows?" Kelsey asked as she sipped her tea. She watched him eat with a smile on her face.

"Sleep," Gene said, laughing.

"You could do that. I won't bother you," Kelsey said with that half smile of hers that drove him crazy. Gene arched one of his eyebrows.

"Do you really think I could sleep knowing you were in the next room?" he asked. "No, I don't think so. Besides, I don't want to waste any of our time together sleeping by myself." He grabbed her and kissed her. Kelsey laughed.

"We could take a drive around town, visit some of our old haunts," Kelsey said as she started cleaning up the breakfast dishes.

"That's a great idea," he said. "We could stop by the cemetery," he continued quietly, sipping the last of his coffee. "His birthday is next week."

Kelsey stopped and turned toward him. "That sounds nice. We've never been there together. It'll be a treat for James, both of his parents there." Kelsey smiled.

* * *

Danny

The whole way home, all he thought about was Kelsey. God, she looked great! He had never told Gene about their time together. It was when he left the band briefly in 1979. Already the "business" had been getting to him. Too much touring, women, booze, and pills. He had just wanted to sing. But he needed to get clean. He had come home to the mountains and rippling waters of Colorado and there she was, so vulnerable. It had been about five years since Kelsey and Gene had broken up. After a few weeks of rest, he started singing at some local festivals with her. They sounded great together. They had always been great friends, nothing physical. Not that he didn't want to, but she had been Gene's girl when he first met her. This time he was going to take his best shot. Whenever they were onstage, they shared a mic. He would hold her close during the love songs. Then they started holding hands and going out when they weren't onstage. He knew he had to take it slow with her. The breakup with Gene had really broken her. He had seen it.

Well, it hadn't worked out the way he wanted. They had kissed a few times, but Kelsey said they were just meant to be friends. Sex would ruin their friendship, she had said. He didn't know about that! He could tell she was trying to get over Gene but was having a hard time. Soon after, he went back to the band. He needed the money and singing was all he knew. He discovered harder drugs this go-around and that helped dull the pain.

CHAPTER SEVEN

*K*elsey and Gene drove all around, visiting all the places they had talked about last night, reliving the memories. Finally, they came to the cemetery. They stayed in the car for a while, then got out together, and held hands as they walked toward James's final resting place.

James Eugene Kelly
Died: August 15, 1974

"You gave him my name for his middle name," Gene said, squeezing her hand. "I'll bet your father wasn't happy about that."

"No, he wasn't." Kelsey replied, "But, I insisted. It was the only thing I fought him on. He and my mom made all the arrangements. I was in pretty bad shape." She sighed as she wiped a tear, remembering. After all these years, thinking about it still made her cry.

They stood there for a few moments, and Kelsey started really crying and yelling at him, "Where were you Gene? You promised to be there! You promised!" Gene went to put his arms around her. Kelsey started punching his chest with her fists then grabbed his shirt. "Why didn't you come, Genie? I needed you! I needed you! I was so scared!" Kelsey ran off to a nearby bench, sat down, put her head in her hands, and continued to cry.

* * *

Gene

He let out a big breath. He sat down beside her. This was it. How was he going to tell her? *How much* should he tell her? He didn't want to tell her the truth: that her parents had kept him away from her and kept them apart for more than a year after, until he just gave up. Gene sat beside her and started rubbing her back.

"Don't touch me!" Kelsey yelled and moved over to the far side of the bench.

"I'm so sorry, Kelsey." Gene said, turning toward her. "Sorry for everything. We were both so young. I tried to get there! You have to believe that! I really tried!" He didn't want to say anything else. He would not be the one to alienate her from her family. They were all very close. He couldn't do that to her.

"But afterward, you didn't even write or call!" Kelsey cried.

* * *

Gene

This was going to be tricky, he thought. He had written. Every week for over a year. He suspected that someone in her family intercepted the mail, and Kelsey never received his letters. He even tried calling a few times. He was told Kelsey wasn't there, or sleeping, or busy and not to call again. He knew she never got any of his messages. She would have talked to him or called him back. After several tries, he gave up. When he was in town, he would try to go to see her and was always stopped by someone in her family. Mostly her father. Mr. Kelly never forgave him for getting Kelsey pregnant and "ruining" his little girl. He had settled for watching her from a distance around town. Finally, he just moved on with his life.

"I...I...I didn't know what to say," he lied. "You had been through so much. I felt so unworthy of you, like it was all my fault! I wish I could have been the man you needed. But I didn't know how!

I know, that sounds really lame." His voice trailed off. He started crying. He hated lying to her.

* * *

Kelsey

She lifted her head and looked at him. She had never even considered his feelings. He had lost a child too. They had both been so young at the time. Barely out of their teens. It was time to move on. Losing baby James was part of God's plan for both of them. It was no one's fault. She moved closer to Gene and put her arms around him.

"I'm sorry, Genie," Kelsey said, hugging him and kissing his tear stained cheek.

"Please forgive me, Kels," Gene said, wiping his eyes.

"I did, baby, a long time ago or I couldn't have moved on with my life," she said. "I hope you can forgive me. You lost a child too."

"Nothing to forgive," he said, relieved. They sat on the bench in front of James's final resting place and held each other, quietly, for a long time after.

Since PJ wasn't going to come home until Gene left, he did. And he took Kelsey with him. They went to spend a few days at his house in the mountains.

Gene was so excited about showing Kelsey his home. He had a few acres with a lake where he went fishing whenever he was home. Fishing was his home away from the world and had been their "thing" when they were younger. They would always meet at the lake by her parents' house after their curfews to be together to go fishing in the dark. In the summer, he would catch something, and Kelsey would cook it over an open fire. He was hoping she would love his home too. Enough to move in someday soon. For him, that's where this relationship was headed. He wasn't about to lose her again.

* * *

Kelsey

She felt funny about going to Gene's without talking to PJ. Let's face it, she felt funny about going to Gene's at all. Was she ready for this relationship? She knew she wanted it. But PJ had made his feelings clear. She was so tired of living her life according to what her son wanted. It would be nice to get away and do something for herself for a change before school starts. Lord knows she was overdue! She would be missing a garden club meeting next week, but those old biddy's never listen to her anyway. She'd come back a week before the start of school and get the music room ready. PJ was going to be doing his student teaching with her this year and taking over for her when she retired.

They pulled up to the house. It was a long log cabin, ranch-style home built into the side of the mountain. On the back of the house, Gene had added a recording studio.

"Gene! It's beautiful!" Kelsey exclaimed. Gene smiled, glad she was pleased. He grabbed their bags and they headed up the front steps. His housekeeper, Maria, opened the door to greet them. He had called her earlier to tell her he was bringing Kelsey home with him.

"Welcome home, Senior Gene!" Maria said, "Who is our guest?"

"Maria, this is Kelsey," he said. "Kelsey, this is my housekeeper/surrogate mother-sister, sometimes a pain in the ass, Maria. She runs this house like a finely tuned car."

"So nice to meet you," Kelsey said, shaking her hand.

"Nice to meet you too," Maria responded. "I like her, Gene!" Gene smiled. This was a good sign, if Maria liked her.

Gene showed her every inch of the property. They spent a lot of time at the lake getting to know each other again. They talked about everything…except James. Kelsey wanted to talk to him about the baby, how scared she had been, the first few years after, but she couldn't bring herself to bring it up. He was so happy. She would wait for the right time.

CHAPTER EIGHT

Kelsey and Gene saw each other few times a week throughout the fall. They also texted several times and day and spoke every night. It was a challenge because in addition to her classes at school, she had rehearsal almost every day after school for the holiday show. Kelsey joined Gene for the few concerts the band had scheduled. He hated being alone after a show, so Kelsey made sure she was always there for him. Most nights she joined the guys onstage for a song or two. She ended up becoming a sort of surrogate mother to all of them. She would mend shirts that needed buttons, offer parenting advise, make sure they all ate right, things like that. Gene always teased her that the guys spent more time with her on the road, then he did. He often drove down to school and helped out with rehearsals too. The kids loved him. He was so patient with them. PJ did not hide his disapproval very well when Gene was around. He made sure Gene knew how he felt about the relationship. Gene didn't say anything to Kelsey. He thought that was her call. But he was getting a little tired of coming in second with her, though. But after all these years, he'd settle for second place until PJ accepted him.

They made plans with Emily to spend Thanksgiving at Gene's house with his son, Declan, and his family. Kelsey and Emily were a little nervous about meeting Gene's family, but he assured them that they would love both of them. PJ was going to Meghan's. Kelsey thought more and more about retiring. This relationship with Gene made her feel like a teenager again. More than once, Kelsey and Gene talked about her moving in with him. Gene wanted her with him all the time. Kelsey was worried about how PJ would react.

"He's a grown man, Kels," Gene said, when they spoke on the phone later that night. "You can't live your life waiting for his approval."

"I know, I know," Kelsey said, sighing. "And I know, I baby him. But he had such a hard time after Pete died."

"It's been five years," he reminded her gently.

"I know, you're right," she said. "I'll have a talk with him after Thanksgiving."

"Maybe you could move in soon?" he asked, hopefully.

"Maybe," she teased. "I love you, Gene." Kelsey said. "I love you more." Gene answered. They said good night with the promise to talk the next day.

CHAPTER NINE

"Hey, Mom," PJ said, the next day as he was cleaning up after dinner. "Meghan wants to know what kind of pie you want her to bring."

Kelsey looked up from the papers she was grading, "Bring?" she asked. "What do you mean? Emily and I are going to Gene's, remember?"

"No, Meghan and her parents are coming to our house," he said, turning from the dishwasher. "Didn't I tell you?"

"No, you didn't!" she exclaimed. "PJ! It's Monday before Thanksgiving! I still have school till Wednesday afternoon! When were you going to tell me?"

"Relax, I'm telling you now. You can do this. You're Super Mom." He smiled that Pete McCoury smile that had always worked in the past. He looked just like his father. "Please? It's really important to Meghan and me to have Thanksgiving with both families." Kelsey sighed, it worked again!

* * *

Kelsey

Oh, she was so mad! How could he do this to her? He knew how much spending time with Gene meant to her. Maybe that's why he did it. He was starting to grudgingly accepted Gene as a part of Kelsey's life but was not happy about it. But she really loved PJ's girlfriend, Meghan and if she was bringing her parents, this relationship was getting serious. Guess she was cooking Thanksgiving dinner! How was she going to tell Gene? Kelsey punched in his number into her phone for their nightly phone call.

"Hey, baby," Gene said cheerfully. "How was your day?"

"Hey, hon," Kelsey answered, "I've had better." Kelsey sighed.

"Oh? Only three days till we see each other. Think you can hang on?" he teased.

"About that…I…ah…won't be able to come for Thanksgiving." Kelsey winced, waiting for the explosion.

"What? I thought it was all set! What happened?" he asked, clearly upset.

"PJ invited Meghan and her parents. I've met them before, but it seems to be important to both of them that we celebrate this Thanksgiving together. I guess they're getting serious," Kelsey said. "Gene, he just told me tonight after dinner! Her parents are coming in tomorrow to spend the week with Meghan. There's nothing I can do! I'm so sorry!"

Gene didn't answer right away. He started counting. One… two…three…PJ, figures. He didn't want to start an argument, but he was really upset by this news. Gene knew PJ was not happy about him and Kelsey. She had been choosing PJ over him for the past three months. So PJ wouldn't be upset. God, she coddled that kid!

"I was really hoping you could meet Declan and his family. I kinda thought we were getting serious too," he said tersely. He knew that was a low blow, but he was feeling sorry for himself.

Kelsey sighed, blinking back tears, feeling pulled in two different directions by the two most important men in her life.

"I know," she said, "I'm sorry, I have to do this for him. He's counting on me."

"Well, I guess I know where I stand." He knew he was being an ass but couldn't stop himself. "Call when you have time for me again." He hung up on her.

* * *

Kelsey

She stared at the phone. Damn him! How dare he hang up on her! She knew he was getting serious. So was she! She liked the idea. She wanted to be there as much as he wanted her there. But to ask her to choose him over her son is totally unfair! Of course, PJ springing the news about Thanksgiving two days before wasn't fair either. Damn both of them!

On Thanksgiving morning, she got up at 5:00 AM to put the turkey in. Dinner was at 2:00 PM. Kelsey cooked all morning—stuffing, mashed potatoes, vegetables, appetizers, desserts. She had made a few pies yesterday afternoon to take to Gene's on Friday. She was planning on driving up to spend the weekend. So far, nothing was stopping those plans! They hadn't spoken since Monday. She had texted him a few times, but the only answer she got was, "Whatever, Kels." God, that man was stubborn!

At 9:00 AM, she got a call from Emily. Emily had decided she didn't want to go to Gene's without Kelsey. Another reason for Gene to be mad at her. Gene and Emily had been seeing each other and speaking on the phone regularly since August. At least that relationship was on solid ground!

"Hi Mom. Happy Thanksgiving." Emily said, her voice drooping.

"Hello, my love, Happy Thanksgiving!" Kelsey said, "Em, you sound tired."

"I was on duty last night and haven't left yet," she said. "I'm sorry, Mom, I won't be able to make dinner today. There was a baby born last night that isn't going to make it. I've been helping her mother go through the grieving process. Mom, I can't leave her. She's just destroyed about the baby. So is the father. We've been taking turns holding the baby until…well, until we don't have to anymore." Emily's voice cracked.

"Oh, Em, I'm so sorry," she said. She certainly knew what that young girl was going through. "Is there anything I can do?"

"No…yes, you can pray…. It shouldn't be long now," Emily said.

"I will. Call me later after you've gotten some sleep, and we'll talk. Kelsey said. "I'll bring over some food. I love you, Em."

"Okay. I love you too, Mommy," Emily said, her voice a little stronger.

"Love you three," Kelsey said, playing their favorite game. She could picture Emily smiling into the phone.

"Love you, four...ever," Emily said as she disconnected the phone. Kelsey bowed her head.

"Heavenly Father, please be with that young couple. Take their baby into your loving arms when the time comes. Hold the parents in your loving arms and give them the strength to deal with their loss. I pray they turn to you for help. In Jesus's name, Amen. Oh, and please help my girl too." Poor Emily! She took her job as a NICU nurse so seriously. Kelsey hopes she doesn't burn herself out.

She texted Gene: *Em's got a tough double shift ahead of her. Patient dying. She's comforting the mother. Hearing your voice would make her feel better. It would make me feel better too.* 🫤. Before she could change her mind, she hit the Send button.

A few minutes later, she gets a text from him, "*Thanks. I'll call her.*" Nothing about calling Kelsey. Oh, that man is infuriating!

At ten thirty, she got a call from Meghan. "Hey, Meg, Happy Thanksgiving," Kelsey said.

"Hi, Mrs. McCoury, Happy Thanksgiving," said Meghan. "I just wanted to apologize, personally, for the change in plans today."

"Change? What change?" asked Kelsey, her heart dropping.

"Didn't PJ tell you?" she said. "My father broke his ankle jumping off his bike on Monday. They're still in Michigan and since they weren't coming, I took an extra shift at the store and will be working today. PJ was going to have dinner with me on my break. He said he would tell you."

"No, he didn't tell me," Kelsey said quietly. "I've been cooking all morning."

"Oh no!" Meghan cried. "He wouldn't let me call you. He insisted on telling you himself!"

"So, when did this happen? Monday? Morning or afternoon?" Kelsey asked.

"Afternoon," Meghan answered.

"Well, at least he didn't lie about everything," Kelsey muttered to herself. "Thank you so much for telling me, Meghan," Kelsey said. "I'm sorry, but I have to hang up now and kill my son!"

Meghan let out a nervous laugh. "Save some of him for me! Maybe you'll be able to go to Gene's after all?"

Kelsey stopped and thought, *Yes, Meghan, I will.* Kelsey smiled at the thought.

* * *

Kelsey

She was so mad she imagined there was white smoke coming out of her ears. How dare he. He had gone too far this time. Very methodically, she turned off the oven, took off her apron, folded it, and put it away in the drawer. She went to her room to pack her weekend bag. When she was finished, she made sure all the perishables were in the fridge but left the dirty dishes all over the counters and in the sink. She put her bag, a plate for Meghan, and two pies in the car. She then wrote a long letter to PJ telling him how disappointed she was in him, how he took her for granted, especially after his father had died. She owned up to her part in enabling him, but that was done. She had more than earned her right to be happy and she was going to be, whether he liked it or not. The second page of the letter was a list of chores she expected him to have done by the time she returned on Sunday night. If she was going to be moving in with Gene, they would have to start getting the house ready to sell. She then filled her best crystal pitcher with the coldest water from the tap and knocked on PJ's door.

"Rise and shine, sleepyhead!" Kelsey said sweetly and poured the water on his head.

"What! What!" he sputtered. "What's happening!" He looked at her questionably, his hair and pajama top all wet.

"Meghan called this morning!" Kelsey shouted. At least he had the decency to look guilty! "There's a note for you in the kitchen, I'm going to Gene's." Not giving him a chance to answer, she stomped out of the house and drove away.

"Shit!" PJ said.

CHAPTER TEN

* * *

Gene

*H*e thought he doing a good job pretending to have a good day. Playing with the grandkids helped. No one noticed that he was miserable. At least he didn't think so. He checked his phone every few minutes. Why would she call? He had been down right mean the last time they spoke and he couldn't bring himself to apologize. He was still very hurt. His heart leaped a little when he got the text about Emily. Kelsey hinted for him to call her too, but he didn't. Why was he being so stubborn? He did talk to Em. His poor girl, going through all that emotion with the young mother. He hoped hearing from him helped.

He wondered if she was still going to come up tomorrow. He hoped so. He wouldn't blame her if she didn't. Of course, if he called her, he would know for sure.

* * *

Kelsey

On the way to Gene's, she stopped at the department store that Meghan worked at and dropped off the plate of food she made. She told Meghan that PJ would be too busy with his list of chores to see her later. Meghan thanked her and promised that PJ would complete the list. She fought back tears the whole ride to Gene's, thinking of this latest stunt of PJ's. She would not arrive at Gene's with swollen eyes! Thinking back on the previous months since reuniting with Gene, she cannot believe how she let PJ manipulate her! She was surprised Gene had put up with it for so long. No wonder he hadn't called or texted her. Well, it stops now. Her number one priority in her life now was herself!

"Grandpa, you sad," said Sophie, stroking Gene's face with her little hand. Sophie, sitting on Gene's lap, was his son, Declan's, three-year-old.

"No, honey," Gene said, trying to smile, "I'm so happy you and Dylan came over for turkey today."

"No, no, you sad," Sophie replied, shaking her head. "Why, Grandpa?"

Gene didn't try to fight it. This kid was smart. He sighed.

"Well, honey," he said, "My friend was supposed to come over today and now she can't." Sophie put her arms around his neck and hugged him. "Poor Grandpa." Gene hugged her back, smiling a little.

"Sophie," Declan called from the doorway, "come over here. I have something that I think will cheer up Grandpa."

"Daddy, Grandpa needs a play date with his friend," Sophie said, jumping down from Gene's lap and scampering over to her father.

"I think that can be arranged. Go find Mommy, honey," Declan said, smiling. Sophie blew a kiss to Gene and left the room.

Gene glanced up toward Declan. "Happy Thanksgiving, Dad," he said and stepped aside. Behind him stood Kelsey. Gene's heart did a flip!

Declan quietly left the room and closed the door behind him. Gene couldn't move. She had come! He just sat there, staring at her.

"Don't just sit there, you big lug," she said, "get up and kiss me!" Gene smiled and did as he was told.

"What happened?" he asked as he hugged her.

"It's a long story," Kelsey answered and hugged him back. "Tighter," she said as she leaned into him. He hugged her tighter. Kelsey sighed with contentment and buried her head in his embrace.

"I'm so sorry, Gene," she said, tears escaping her eyes and running down his neck.

"It's okay, baby," he answered, holding her close. He handed her his handkerchief from his back pocket. Kelsey wiped her eyes and Gene hugged her again. "I'm sorry too." She smiled at him.

"How long till dinner?" Kelsey asked as she started kissing his neck.

"'Bout half an hour," he answered, enjoying every minute.

"That's enough time," she said with a smile on her face. "Why don't you take my bag up to your room so I can unpack and we can...um...you know."

Before she could finish the sentence, Gene opened the door of the living room, grabbed her bag, her hand, ran through the kitchen to the stairs, and bounded up the steps two at a time. Kelsey followed, laughing.

They came down thirty minutes later looking very happy. "Grandpa, you smile!" said Sophie.

"That's right, baby girl, Grandpa very happy now! Did you meet my friend?" he asked, introducing Kelsey.

"How do you do, Sophie?" Kelsey said, extending her hand. "I've heard a lot about you."

"I like you, you make Grandpa smile!" she said. Everyone laughed and sat down to dinner.

Once everyone was served and had started eating, Declan asked about how she had ended up coming to dinner after all.

"Well," Kelsey began. "I suppose I'll laugh about it one day." She recounted all that had happened since PJ had told her on Monday of Meghan's parents coming to dinner to leaving the house this afternoon.

"Wow," Declan said, stunned. "And you let him live?" That got a laugh from everyone. "Can't wait to meet this kid!"

After dinner, Kelsey and Gene went for a walk by the lake.

"Hey," she said, squeezing his hand, "I'm giving serious thought to retiring. Are you still serious about me moving in with you?"

"You bet! You don't even have to go home Sunday!" He said excitedly, hugging her.

"Gene! I have to go home on Sunday!" she said, laughing. "I was thinking after Christmas. I have a lot to do to get the house ready to sell."

"Tell me what I can do to help. Anything to speed up the process!" He picked her up and swung her around. She had just made him the happiest man in the world!

CHAPTER ELEVEN

*T*ime between Thanksgiving and Christmas just seemed to evaporate. Kelsey was so busy with the holiday show at school and being with Gene at his concerts that she hadn't even begun to get the house ready for sale. Gene really loved having Kelsey at the shows with him. She was exhausted. She would have to find the time in the new year.

* * *

Danny

He had been so happy these past few months since Kelsey came back into his life. Well, really Gene's life, but he and Gene were best friends and lived across the lake from each other. He knew when she was at Gene's house. He didn't make a pest of himself, but he saw enough of Kelsey to cut out the drugs and cut back on the drinking. Kelsey invited him over for dinner quite often. She knew he lived alone and probably wasn't eating right. Maybe he hinted that to her in casual conversation. Right after Thanksgiving, she had come to him for help on a Christmas present for Gene. She had written Gene a song and wanted to record it. He offered the use of his studio and even played some of the instruments. It was a great song. She really should release it as a single. Kelsey could be a big star, if she wanted, but she wouldn't hear of it. This song was for Gene. It didn't matter to him. He just loved spending time with her. He even had PJ video-tape the recording session. It would be ready for Christmas.

* * *

Kelsey

She was so excited about this present for Gene. This was her first try at serious song writing. She had written a lot of simple stuff for school productions, but Danny said this could be a bona fide hit! Not that she cared. Kelsey wanted this song for Gene and Gene alone. They had put the finishing touches on it last week. It was perfect!

One week till Christmas! Kelsey couldn't wait! Maybe with some rest she could finally shake this cold that had been plaguing her since the middle of December. She was spending Christmas with Gene and Declan and his family. They were all flying to Nashville on Christmas Eve. Declan's wife, Karen's parents lived outside Nashville. They would spend Christmas Day with them and go to a party later on to take care of some contract negotiations for the Bluebird cafe. Declan and Gene were expanding their skills to include producing shows. Karen and the kids would get a nice long visit with her parents. Emily was working and PJ was going to Michigan to see Meghan's family. He had been good as gold since Thanksgiving. Everything on the list she had left him was done and the kitchen was sparkling clean when she got back.

God, she was tired! This cold was making its way all over her body. She just had to hang on.

"Okay, everyone! Places!" Kelsey called, clapping her hands. "Showtime in ten minutes."

The holiday show was one of the highlights for the kids who attended the Woodhaven School for Special Needs. The school had evolved over the years. Her parents had started the school for Kelsey's older sister, Alice, who was born with Down Syndrome. Her parents had found very little in the way of education for Alice. So they started their own school with private funding. It had started with students with Down Syndrome. Over the years, they had expanded to include students on the autistic spectrum as well. Unfortunately, Alice's physical health had been very poor and died of pneumonia at the age of ten. Kelsey's job in the Music Department was to use music to help them with their other subjects at school and life in the mainstream world. For instance, this year she had a student who had come to them as a high functioning autistic and a selective mute. She had started out using sign language as a third grader and now as a senior, ready to graduate, she was singing in front of the whole school!

The show went off without a hitch. Her family was all there. Everyone except her father. Unfortunately, he was only lucid in the morning. Gene and Danny were there too. She was so proud of her kids! PJ had been a great help with all aspects of the show. He was ready. She was leaving her students in good hands. It wasn't public knowledge yet, but she had officially put in her retirement papers with the principal of the school last week. She and PJ were going to tell the kids together after the Christmas break. She couldn't wait to get home and collapse!

Christmas Eve morning

"Mom, Mom, wake up! You overslept," PJ said, shaking her gently. "Don't you have to leave for Gene's this morning?"

Kelsey opened her eyes. Her head felt like a ton of bricks! She swallowed. It felt like she was swallowing glass! *Oh, that hurt!*

"What time is it?" she croaked. She couldn't even talk! PJ felt her forehead. It was more than a little warm.

"Mom, you're burning up. You've got a fever. Stay in bed, I'll get the thermometer," he said, rushing to the bathroom. He placed the thermometer in her ear. "102.9, not good. You need to see a doctor," PJ said. "I'll call Emily. Maybe Conrad can stop by." Conrad was Dr. Conrad Matthews, Emily's new boyfriend and a third-year resident.

"No...no...don't bother them. They're both working the emergency room today," Kelsey whispered, trying to get out of bed. "I'll just take some Tylenol, I'll be fine." Kelsey had been looking forward to this time with Gene for too long. A little sore throat and fever were not going to stop her. The next thing she knew, PJ was tapping her face trying to wake her up.

"Mom…Mom…you fainted! Get back in bed! I'm calling Conrad!" PJ commanded. PJ helped her back under the covers before dialing Emily's phone number. Emily and Conrad came right over. Conrad examined her. Kelsey's fever was now 103.5. Her throat was almost swollen shut and congestion had started building in her chest.

"I'm sorry, Mrs. McCoury, but you are very sick. You are not going anywhere for at least a week," Dr. Matthews said with authority. Problem was he looked like he was twelve years old.

"Forget it," Kelsey whispered. "I have to drive to Gene's today and we're flying to Nashville tonight."

"No, you're not," he said again, very sternly. "You are a very sick person and very contagious right now. If you don't take care of this, you're looking a pneumonia in a few days."

Kelsey lay back on her pillows resigned and ready to cry. "Emily, would you call Gene for me?" she whispered.

"Of course, Mom," she answered, picking up her phone.

"I'm going to call in some meds to the pharmacy and schedule you for a chest x-ray after the holiday." Conrad continued. Kelsey nodded, tears running down her cheeks. Conrad felt so bad! He patted her hand. "I'm really sorry," he said. He felt terrible.

"Hey, little girl," Gene said when he saw Emily's picture pop up on his phone. "Is your mom on her way up?"

"Hey, Gene," Emily answered. She dreaded telling him. "Gene, Mom is really sick and won't be able to come up for Christmas or go to Nashville." She told him what condition Kelsey was in when she woke up this morning and Conrad's diagnosis.

"What? She told me it was just a bad cold!" he said, alarmed.

"Up until this morning, it probably was," Emily said.

"Tell Kelsey, I'm coming. I'm leaving now." Gene was about to hang up the phone and jump in the car.

"No, don't come down, she's very contagious. It will be a few days before you can see her."

Shit! "Can I talk to her?" Gene asked.

"Of course. We'll Facetime. Mom? Gene's on the phone," Emily said, turning the phone toward Kelsey.

"Kelsey, honey, what's going on? Are you all right?" he asked. She looked miserable!

"So sorry, Gene," Kelsey whispered.

"Oh man! You can't even talk. Listen, I'm not going. I'll wait till you're not contagious anymore, come down and take care of you. I want to see you through this."

Kelsey shook her head. "Go," she whispered. "Important to you and Declan." She pushed the phone away. She didn't want Gene to see her cry.

Emily took the phone. "She wants you to go, Gene," Emily said. "It'll be fine. Between PJ and I, we'll take good care of her."

* * *

Gene

He did not want to leave town with Kelsey so sick. He had a funny feeling in the pit of his stomach. He worried the rest of the day. Should he go? Declan was counting on this production deal so he could spend more time with his family and less time on the road. Should he stay? Last time he left Kelsey when she was sick, he lost her for over 30 years! Of course, it's not the same circumstances, but he couldn't shake that nagging feeling that he should stay.

Chapter Twelve

Christmas day, around 3 PM

"Come on, Em. Pick up...pick up!" PJ said desperately into his cell phone.

"Hey, Bro, what's up? How's Mom?" Emily said when she answered the phone.

"Em, I can't wake Mom! She won't wake up!" PJ cried.

"Is she breathing? PJ, Is she breathing?" Emily asked, alarmed.

"Yes, she's breathing, but it doesn't sound right." PJ said.

"Call 911, get an ambulance and get her to the hospital!" Emily yelled into the phone. "I'll meet you in the ER! PJ, did you hear me?"

"Em. I'm scared!" PJ whispered.

"Be scared later! Mom needs you!" Emily yelled. "Call 911!"

* * *

Emily

After hanging up with PJ, she started shaking. Stop it! Get a hold of yourself! Mom needs you! She took a deep breath and walked to the chapel in the hospital. She knelt and made the sign of the cross. "Dear Lord," she prayed, "please, please, not yet. Don't take her yet. Help me to be strong for her, Lord. Amen." Then she texted Conrad and asked him to meet her at the entrance of the emergency room. She explained to him what was happening while they waited for her mother's ambulance. She would call Gene when she knew more.

* * *

Gene

He wished he didn't have to be here at this party. All he could think about was Kelsey home in bed, sick as a dog. But it was important to the contract negotiations to "network" and "be seen." He hadn't been able to call Emily since this morning and was worried about Kelsey. That pit in his stomach hadn't gone away. In fact, it had gotten bigger. He felt his phone vibrate. It was Emily!

"Gene?" Emily said, her voice cracking a little.

"What? Em, is she any better?" Gene asked, hearing her voice, fearing the worst.

"PJ found her around three o'clock, unconscious," Emily said, her voice wavering. "We got her to the hospital. She has pneumonia, a throat infection, and a raging fever. Everything is treatable. The problem is her fever. It's spiked to 105, and we can't get it to break. She's hallucinating," Emily said, starting to cry.

Gene felt his body fall into a chair. He put his head in his hand. He knew he should have stayed. "She'll probably be fine," Emily continued, "make a full recovery, but her older sister Alice, the one with Down Syndrome, died of pneumonia. She was only ten. I know it's not the same. Medical advances and..." Emily said, "but, Gene... Dad... I'm scared." Emily whispered the last two words.

"Emily, I'm on my way. You stay strong, my girl, I *will* be there. What hospital?" he asked. He wrote the name of the hospital on a cocktail napkin. "I'll text you when I'm in route. I love you, Em," he said, hanging up. She called him Dad! Gene said a silent prayer to God and Pete McCoury asking for the strength to be worthy of her.

Declan had been watching his father while he was talking on his phone and quickly went over to him. "Dad, what is it? What's wrong?" he asked. He put his hand on Gene's shoulder.

"It's Kelsey." Gene said. "She's in the hospital. PJ found her unconscious. Listen, son," he said, standing and clutching Jeff's shirt. "I have to get to her. I have to be there. You'll have to handle the contracts yourself."

"Dad, it's okay, it'll be okay," he reassured him, covering Gene's hands with his. "We'll get you home. It might take a day or two but—"

"No!" Gene interrupted. "I have to get there *now*! You don't understand!" Gene shouted, "I have to be there. I wasn't there last time, and I lost her! I have to get back to Colorado *now*! I won't lose her again!" Declan looked at his father. Gene looked stricken! He had never seen him this upset. Something else was going on here. He sat Gene down in a chair and tried to think.

"Excuse me, can I be of some help? I couldn't help overhear," said Mort Solomon, one of the investors in the Bluebird Cafe and who they were in negotiations with about producing shows. Declan briefly explained the situation at home and why Gene needed to get back there as soon as possible.

"How about a private plane? Could probably get you there in three to four hours," Mort said. Gene looked at Mort with gratitude. "Be at the Nashville airport in an hour. I'll have the plane ready to go." Declan and Gene looked at each other, not able to believe their good fortune! "Thank you, Mr. Solomon!" said Gene, gratefully shaking his hand. "Thank you!"

"Think nothing of it. I know what you're going through. And call me Mort," he said. "Now, get going!" Gene left for the hotel to get his luggage. Declan called Emily to get the details of Kelsey's condition and to tell her Gene was on his way.

Gene texted Emily three and a half hours later to tell her his plane was landing. He called her from the Uber.

"How is she?" he asked.

"About the same," Emily said, her voice trembling. "Her fever is still high. She keeps mumbling about 'her baby.' 'Want my baby,' she keeps saying. 'Where's Gene?' 'Where's my sweet baby?' When I tell her you're on your way, she shakes her head and says 'No, he's not coming,' 'he's not here.' Then she starts crying again. Gene, what baby? Do you know what she's talking about?"

* * *

Gene

He sighed. He knew all too well. Kelsey was reliving losing James all over again. Despite what Kelsey believed, he *had* finally mad it to the hospital after she lost the baby.

"Yes, I do honey." He said, quietly. "I'll be there soon." When the cab reached the hospital, Gene jumped out and rushed inside to the elevator.

When the elevator door opened, Gene rushed into the waiting area outside Kelsey's room. Dr. Matthews, Emily and PJ were sitting together, looking very serious. PJ and Conrad were both holding Emily's hands. Where was Kelsey's family? Gene expected them to be here for her.

"Let me see her. I can help," he said to Conrad. "I know what to do."

Conrad frowned. Gene wasn't family. "I'm sorry, Gene, technically, you're not family. Only family can see Mrs. McCoury." But Emily overruled him, and PJ helped him into the blue gown with a surgical mask. Conrad relented and took him to Kelsey's room.

Kelsey's room was softly lit. Her nurse, Nancy, stood by her bed, holding Kelsey's hand. Gene sucked in his breath at the site of Kelsey. She was drenched in sweat, tossing and turning, muttering about the baby and him. It was just like forty years ago. This time he wasn't going to let her down.

"Nancy, this is Gene, Mrs. McCoury's fiancé," Conrad said. "Give him whatever assistance he needs. He's here to help. What's her condition now?" Conrad checked Kelsey's chart. Nancy's eyes grew big. Oh my god, Gene Miller from the FyreByrds! Her parents were huge fans!

"She's about the same, Dr. Matthews. Fever is still 105 and the hallucinations are getting worse," Nancy said.

"What are you still doing here, Nancy?" Conrad asked, glancing at her. "Your shift was over hours ago."

"I'm not leaving until her fever breaks," Nancy said. Nancy's younger brother had attended the Woodhaven School and Kelsey had been a tremendous help to him. She even got him a job after he graduated. Nancy wasn't leaving until Kelsey was out of danger.

"Well, get someone to spell you and get some sleep," Conrad said.

"Yes, Doctor," Nancy said.

"Nancy," Gene said, "I need to get into bed with Kelsey. Will you help me?"

Nancy look questioningly at Conrad, who nodded his head.

"Text me her vitals every thirty minutes," Conrad said as he left the room. Nancy helped Gene into the hospital bed and pulled up the guard rail.

Gene took Kelsey in his arms. "I'm here, baby, I'm here," he murmured in her ear. She fought him. "No…no…want my baby… where's Gene?" She kept hitting him.

"Kelsey, I'm here, baby," he said again, wrapping his arms around her tighter.

"No…no…not coming. Mom said…too busy…doesn't care. I need Gene!" Kelsey started crying and hitting Gene with her fists.

Gene started singing, softly, in her ear. A song that meant so much to both of them. When they found out Kelsey was pregnant and if it was a boy, they wanted to name him James after the James Taylor song Sweet Baby James, that was popular at the time. Gene sang it to her and her belly every night. He even sang to her when he called from the road.

> There is a young cowboy, he lives on the range
> His horse and his cattle are his only companions
> He works in the saddle and sleeps in the canyons
> Waiting for summer, his pastures to change
> And as the moon rises he sits by the fire
> Thinking about women and glasses of beer

And closing his eyes as the doggies retire
He sings out a song which is soft but it's clear
As if maybe someone could hear

Goodnight you moonlight ladies
Rockabye sweet baby James
Deep greens and blues are the colors I choose
Won't you let me go down in my dreams
And rockabye sweet baby James

Now the first of December was covered with
snow
So was the turnpike from Stockbridge to Boston
The Berkshires seemed dreamlike on account of
the frosting
With ten miles behind me and ten thousand
more to go

There's a song that they sing when they take to
the highway
A song that they sing when they take to the sea
A song that they sing of their home in the sky
Maybe you can believe it if it helps you to sleep
But singing works just fine for me

So goodnight you moonlight ladies
Rockabye sweet baby James
Deep greens and blues are the colors I choose
Won't you let me go down in my dreams
And rockabye sweet baby James.
Rockabye sweet baby James

Gene had sung the song several times when Kelsey finally stopped struggling and slumped against him. Her breathing was still very jagged, but she seemed calmer. Her body relaxed more and more with each verse. After about twenty minutes, she sat straight up.

CHAPTER THIRTEEN

"What's happening? Where am I?" Kelsey said, looking around. "Why am I all wet?"

"You're in the hospital, Mrs. McCoury," said Nancy, jumping from her chair and rushing over to the bed. "You have a fever. You're very sick."

Kelsey looked around and saw Gene in bed next to her. She pulled down his surgical mask. Her eyes got very wide. "You *are* here! Gene, you're here! I thought I was dreaming." She laid back down next to him and still staring at him. "You're here," she whispered, touching his face. "You're really here."

"Yes, I am," he whispered back, "and I'll never leave you again." He stroked her cheek and she slumped against him.

Nancy took Kelsey's temperature. "It broke! It's down to 102."

"How did I end up here?" Kelsey asked him.

"I'll tell you later," Gene said, stroking her hair. "Rest now."

Nancy would never have believed it if she hadn't seen it with her own eyes. After all the medicine and ice packs they gave her, all it took to calm her and break the fever was a special song from someone who she guessed was a very special man. She texted Conrad to come right away. While they waited for the doctor, Nancy changed Kelsey's hospital gown. Once they were settled in the bed again, Gene started to sing again. Kelsey sighed with contentment. All of a sudden, it hit her! This had happened before! Kelsey raised her head and looked at Gene. She remembered.

"You *were* there! When I lost James. You held me in the hospital bed, just like now. You sang that song to me! Yes, you were there!" She sat up, remembering it so clearly now. "My mother told me it was probably a dream, that I imagined it. But I didn't. You *were* there." Kelsey lay back down with her head on his chest. "You kept your promise, Genie. You kept your promise."

"Yes, baby," Gene said, pushing her hair behind her ears. "I was there. I promised to be there, and I was."

"But, how? My family told me…I'm confused!" she said.

"I'll tell you all about it when you're feeling better," Gene said. "Close your eyes."

"No, I want to keep looking at you, so you don't disappear." Kelsey smiled weakly and laid her chin on Gene's chest. He smiled back at her. Soon her eyes drooped and closed. She laid her head on his chest and sighed.

Conrad, Emily, and PJ rushed into the room. While Conrad checked the chart and conferred with Nancy, Emily, and PJ gathered around Kelsey's bed. Emily held Kelsey's hand. PJ stood at the end of the bed and looked at Kelsey with tears in his eyes.

He looked at Gene and mouthed, "Thank you." Gene smiled at him and nodded his head.

"Looks like your mother will make a full recovery," Conrad said, very pleased. He smiled at Gene. "Nancy says you worked a miracle, Gene,"

"I just did what I do best," Gene said. He was still holding Kelsey with no intention of letting go.

"Mrs. McCoury, Nancy is going to give you something so you can sleep." Conrad explained, "When you wake, we'll talk more about your condition and your recovery process."

"Can Gene stay till I'm asleep?" she asked. Conrad nodded.

"I'm not going anywhere, baby," he answered.

Nancy injected the drug into her IV and Kelsey fell asleep a few minutes later. PJ and Emily left the room. Conrad wanted to talk to all of them in the waiting area about Kelsey's prognosis.

"Take a few minutes, we'll wait for you outside," Conrad said.

"Thanks, Doc," Gene said.

When he was sure Kelsey was asleep, he motioned for Nancy to come over.

"I'm going to need some help." Gene said to her, "My arm and my leg are both asleep."

Nancy smiled. She wasn't surprised. He had been lying in the same position for over an hour now.

"Okay, we'll take this one step at a time," Nancy said. She put down the guard rail, helped him out of bed and over to a chair. Nancy instructed Gene to keep moving his arm while she massaged his leg to get the circulation going.

"Are you going home now?" Gene asked her. He hoped not, although he knew she had been on almost sixteen hours. It was now around 2:00 AM.

"My next shift starts at 7 AM. I'll go to the rooms to get some sleep and check back later," she said. "How is your arm?"

"Good as new," he said, "the leg too. Thank you, Nancy for your help. You went above and beyond." Gene squeezed her hand.

"Well, Mrs. McCoury means a lot to me and my family." Nancy said. She explained to Gene about her brother. Nancy's fiancé was a teacher at Woodhaven. Kelsey had introduced them. They were getting married in May.

"Mr. Miller? Could I ask a favor?" she asked, shyly.

"Call me Gene and of course," he said.

"My parents are huge fans," she said, a little embarrassed. "If I bring back a CD, would you sign it for me?"

"I'd be happy to. But, let me take care of the CD," he said. "I'll have something here in the next day or two."

"Thank you!" she cried. "My mom is going to flip!"

* * *

Gene

What a sweet girl! He'd have to call Danny and have him bring a bunch of FyreByrds merchandise to sign for her parents. It was the least he could do. Right now he needs to go talk to the doctor about

Kelsey. He took one more look at her before he left the room. She was sleeping so peacefully and cool to the touch. He breathed a sigh of relief as he stroked her cheek.

In the waiting area Gene saw Emily and PJ talking to Conrad. He went to join them.

"...should recover completely," Conrad was saying as Gene came over to them. "Hey, Gene, have a seat."

"Em can fill you in on what we already discussed." Conrad said, "My real concern is her care after she is released. She is going to need full-time care for a few weeks. Full recovery is probably going to take six weeks."

"Wow," PJ said, looking a little scared. "I'm supposed to take over her classes in the new year. Does her health coverage supply nursing?"

"It's okay," Emily said, "I'll take a leave of absence and take care of her myself."

"No, Em, you can't, you have school," PJ said. "You know Mom would never let you skip a semester of school. I think we should hire a nurse."

Gene listened as they argued over how they were going to care for their mother.

"May I say something?" he asked. "How about if I take Kelsey to my house? The band doesn't have another show until almost the end of February. My housekeeper, Maria is available to help me. You guys can call her and come up and see her whenever you want." He waited. He really hoped they would say yes.

"That's actually not a bad idea." PJ said, "Mom was going to move there in the new year anyway."

"I think it's brilliant," Conrad said.

"Gene, are you sure?" Emily said, "It can be very taxing taking care of someone who's so sick."

"I'll have Maria and you guys will help, right?" He asked. They both nodded.

"It's settled," he said. "I'll talk to Nancy about any special equipment we may need."

PJ sat back on the couch, clearly relieved. Emily still looked like she had the weight of the world on her shoulders.

"Speaking of Nancy," Emily said, starting to get up, "Let me go sit with Mom so Nancy can get some sleep."

"I already sent another nurse in there," Conrad said to her, pulling her back down. "All three of you need some sleep." Conrad squeezed her hand. Emily smiled and looked at Conrad with love and gratitude.

"You guys go home," Gene said. "I'll nap in the chair in Kelsey's room. I don't leave until she does." The look he gave them all was very determined. No one argued with him.

Nancy came back in around 7:00 AM. She saw Gene sleeping in the chair. He thought *she* was dedicated! She bustled around the room, checking Kelsey's vitals straightening blankets, adjusting the shades on the windows. Gene woke up around seven thirty.

"Good morning, Gene," Nancy said. "How did you sleep?"

"I'm fine, how is she?" Gene asked, stretching the kink out of his neck. He leaned forward to take Kelsey's hand.

"She's in good shape," Nancy answered. "Her vitals are good, and her breathing is getting better. Why don't you go for a walk and stretch your legs, maybe get some breakfast. Em just got here. She's outside in the waiting area."

"Breakfast with my daughter sounds good," he said, smiling. He kissed Kelsey on the cheek and left the room.

In the waiting area, he found Emily on her phone. She was just hanging up as he approached her.

"Hey, sweetheart," he said as he kissed her cheek.

"Morning," Emily said, returning the kiss.

"Let's get some breakfast. Your Mom's in good hands," Gene said.

"Okay. I'll text PJ to meet us in the cafeteria," Emily said, picking up her phone again.

When they were all settled at a table in the cafeteria, Gene asked Emily the question that had been bothering him since last night.

"Where is your family?" he asked. "Why aren't they here to help you and PJ through this?"

"That's a good question," she said. "After I spoke to you last night, I called Uncle Jerry to ask him to tell everyone else. He said he would. Then he asked me if I had spoken to you yet. I told him, of course, you were the first one I called. He mumbled something about being too busy at work and not able to come. He would pray for my mother. Now, that's weird, right?" Emily looked at him.

"Yes, it is," said PJ, clearly confused by his uncle's attitude. "What do you think, Gene?"

* * *

Gene

Goddamn that Jerry Kelly! How dare he abandon his sister to avoid a confrontation with him! Jerry had been part of the conspiracy that kept him and Kelsey apart when they were younger, and he knew Gene knew this.

"Well, I think I know why your Uncle Jerry isn't here and didn't tell the rest of the family. I think both of you are old enough to hear the truth. Kelsey and I wanted to tell you together, but I think she'll forgive me," Gene said. "When your mom was nineteen, we got pregnant..." Gene told them the whole story, about the stillbirth, about being kept away from Kelsey in the hospital, the unanswered letters, and phone calls. And that their Uncle Jerry, Uncle Robert, and Aunt Sandra were all part of their parents plan to keep Kelsey and Gene apart.

"Kelsey doesn't know about the letters and phone calls, but I think she'll figure it out." Gene said. "She's going to need your support." Emily and PJ nodded, shocked and surprised by the story.

"I forgave them a long time ago." Gene said. "Your grandfather ruled that family with an iron fist. I'm sure no one had a choice but to go along.

"Wow...that answers lot of questions for me and why no one is here," Emily said. "I just spoke with Aunt Toni. She said Jerry never called her. I gave her an update on Mom's condition. She'll let everyone else know and be here this afternoon." Except for Jerry and Toni, Kelsey's brothers and sisters were spread out all over the state of Colorado. Gene guesses their father had a lot to do with *that*.

CHAPTER FOURTEEN

* * *

Danny

*H*e arrived at the hospital around 10:00 AM. He found Gene dozing on the couch outside Kelsey's room. He'd be willing to bet money that Gene hadn't left Kelsey's side since he got there yesterday. He thought back forty years to when they lost their baby. The band was on the other side of Colorado, playing a concert, when their booking agent called with the news. Gene was beside himself trying to find a way home. Kevin decided to drive Gene back home. It took all night.

"Hey, buddy," Danny said to Gene, sitting down next to him. "How's it going? How's Kelsey?" Gene had called Danny earlier this morning and told him about Kelsey. He asked him to bring some FyreByrds stuff to the hospital to sign for Nancy and her family.

"Hey, Danny! She's getting better," Gene said. "Did you bring everything?"

"Yes, I did," Danny replied, handing him a huge paper bag. "They just need to be signed."

"Great! Nancy's family is going to love this!" he said, smiling, looking inside the bag. "Kelsey is coming to the house to recover when she's released. I could use some help, buddy."

"You got it!" Danny said. "You know I'd do anything for Kelsey. You too!" Danny laughed at his own joke.

Gene and Danny took the bag into Kelsey's room. They spent the next hour visiting with Kelsey and signing everything.

"Here, Nancy," he said, handing Nancy the paper bag when she walked in the room later on. "This is for you and your parents." Nancy looked in the bag. It was filled with various FyreByrds merchandise, all signed by Gene and Danny. She beamed at them.

"You know'" she said. "I am going to be golden with them for the rest of my life now!

"You're already golden with me!" he replied, smiling at her with gratitude.

Later on that afternoon, Gene was sitting in the waiting area, checking his phone, when Kelsey's sister, Toni, arrived. Nancy and Emily were taking care of Kelsey at the moment.

"Gene, how is she?" Toni said, hugging him.

"Hey, Toni," Gene answered, hugging her back. "She's turned the corner. Her fever broke early this morning. Still got a ways to go, but she's better." He thought back to when Kelsey lost James. Toni was the one who had called his booking agent to tell him of the still-birth and with the help on one of the nurses, sneaked him in to see Kelsey, and held James's body.

"You look so tired," she said, putting her hand to the side of his face. "Have you been here all night? Go home and get some rest. I'll stay with her."

"I'm fine," he said. "I'm not leaving her again. Kelsey and I go home together." They looked at each other, remembering. Toni wonders if she'll ever find someone to love her the way Gene loves her sister.

"Okay," she said, knowing it would be useless to argue with him. "Can I see her?"

"Of course. Nancy and Emily should be out soon. Sit," he said, pointing to the couch. "Where's your mother?" he asked. He was sure Evelyn would have been here by now.

"She's sick herself or she would have been here last night, if Jerry had bothered to called us!" Toni was furious with her brother.

"Listen, before you see her," Gene said. "Kelsey knows I was with her that night she lost the baby. I don't think it will be long before she figures everything else out. If she asks you, tell her the truth."

"You're right," Toni said. "It's time she knew."

CHAPTER FIFTEEN

* * *

Kelsey

When she woke, she wasn't sure where she was at first. That's right, the hospital, she thought. The last thing she remembered was crying herself to sleep in her own bed after talking to Gene on Christmas Eve. She thought back to when the fever broke and how she had remembered Gene had been with her when she lost James. She went back forty years and thought about her time in the hospital and after she was home again. Why had her mother and father been so adamant that Gene didn't care enough to be with her when she needed him? He had always been there before. They knew he loved her. As she thought about that time, several things did not make sense. They told her Gene never called or wrote. Thinking back, that first year after, she realized that she never had to answer the phone. Whenever it rang, someone else answered. And the mail was always on the desk in the hall when she got home. She never had to go to the mailbox. Why didn't she ask more questions? Why didn't she try to contact Gene herself? She had been severely depressed for a good year after the loss of the baby. She hadn't been strong enough to fight them.

"Hey! There's my favorite sister!" Toni called as she walked into Kelsey's room. "How are you doing, honey?" Toni bent down to hug her.

"Toni! I was wondering when someone from the family would show up!" Kelsey said, happy to see her. "I'm glad it was you." As well as being close as sisters, Toni and Kelsey were very close in age. They were "Irish twins" only eleven months apart. "The others have been acting so strange toward me since I started seeing Gene." Toni looked away. She busied herself by pulling up a chair to Kelsey's bed.

"Toni, tell me what happened when I lost the baby." Kelsey said. "I think I figured it out, but I need confirmation."

Toni sighed. "Okay, here's what happened." Toni told her everything. Their parents decided since the baby was dead, there was no reason for Kelsey and Gene to be together anymore. Under no circumstances was anyone to contact Gene and tell him about the baby. Kelsey and Gene weren't married, he really had no right to be there, Kelsey was a minor. Jerry, Robert, Sandra, and Toni were enlisted to help with the plan. The younger siblings were told that the baby went to heaven, and Kelsey and Gene thought it best that they break up. They were also instructed not to mention Gene's name in front of Kelsey again.

"I thought Mom and Dad were wrong," Toni said. "Gene had every right to be there. Married or not, he was still James's father. I got through to the booking agent and he got a hold of Gene. Kevin drove all night to get Gene to the hospital."

With the help of a sympathetic nurse, they were able to sneak Gene into the room next to Kelsey's so he could hold his son's body and say goodbye. Toni had watched Gene cry as he sang to the baby. After her parents had left for the night, they sneaked Gene into Kelsey's room. He held her and sang to her. Toni wasn't sure if Kelsey had been aware, but she knew Gene needed to be there.

"Mom told me I imagined it, that Gene wasn't there," Kelsey said. Toni sighed. "It came back to me while I had the fever. He got into bed with me and sang James's song. That's when my fever finally broke."

"I'm so sorry, Kels!" Toni cried, "I should have been stronger for you. But you know, Dad, it was hard to fight him on anything!" Toni dissolved in tears. Kelsey leaned over to hug Toni.

Toni wiped her eyes. "After you got home. Jerry, Robert and Sandy were in charge of keeping you and Gene apart. The mail and the phone calls. I refused to be a part of it. I left for college a few days later. I couldn't watch what they were doing to you." Toni grabbed Kelsey's hands. "Can you ever forgive me?"

* * *

Kelsey

She looked at Toni and saw the young eighteen-year-old girl who cried with her in the hospital forty years ago. She could forgive her. She's not sure she could forgive Sandy, Robert, or Jerry. Her parents? They were in their nineties now. Her father was in the full throes of Alzheimer's. He probably didn't even remember. She would have to think about it.

"Of course, I forgive you," Kelsey said. "Listen, I need your help. I need you to take over with Mom and Dad, you know, taking care of them. It looks like I'll be laid up for a while!" Kelsey's parents lived in an assisted living apartment for the past ten years. Of all of them, Kelsey was the one who had taken charge of them after Pete died, doctor's appointments, shopping, etc.

"Don't worry, I can handle it," Toni said. "I've been offering for years to help you."

"And when I am well enough, I want a meeting with the others," she said. "Things are going to change."

Danny and Gene were sitting with Kelsey after dinner, later that day, making plans for her recovery at his home.

"Danny? Would you give me and Gene a minute?" Kelsey asked. She wanted to talk to Gene about what Toni had told her.

"Of course, my queen." Danny smiled, kissed her hand. Kelsey "knighted" him with her fork and he left the room laughing.

"Gene," Kelsey began. "Toni told me everything. How my family kept you away from me and cut off all contact after I lost James." Gene looked down, sorry she had to know the truth.

"I'm sorry, Kels," Gene said. "Sorry it happened and sorry for the way you had to found out. Sorry I wasn't stronger."

"We were both victims, Gene," Kelsey said. "I'm not sure what they did was right. Maybe we would have broken up anyway…probably would have, and gone on to live the lives we had. I don't know. I just wish we could have made that decision." Gene took her hand. "I do know it will be a long time before I can forgive them." Kelsey continued, looking away from Gene. "That first year after. It was the worst of my life. I was so depressed, despondent. Some days I couldn't even get out of bed." Kelsey gulped back tears. "I missed you so much. I really needed my best friend." Kelsey smiled at him through the tears and covered his hand with hers.

Gene smiled back, his eyes glistening. "Me too."

"I may want to talk about it now and then," she said. "Would that be okay?"

"Very okay," Gene said, giving her hand a squeeze.

Chapter Sixteen

New Year's Eve

Kelsey had been discharged from the hospital and was recuperating at Gene's house a few days now. Gene had never been happier. Maria was a big help, but Gene did most of what was required in taking care of her. Kelsey slept a lot. And coughed a lot. Conrad said that was necessary to get all the mucus out of her lungs. It killed him when she cough because she was in so much pain! All he could do was hold her until it was over. But with every day, she got better.

Tonight they were actually going to be alone. PJ and Emily had been here the first few days to help Kelsey get settled. Kelsey insisted they get back to their lives and go ahead with whatever plans they had for the holiday.

"Gene, can I talk to you?" PJ asked New Year's Eve morning. Emily was packing and spending a few moments with her mother before they left.

"Sure, PJ." Gene said, putting his hand on PJ's shoulder. "What's up?" PJ had been very helpful to Gene and Maria in getting Kelsey settled. He did anything that was asked of him. He had also been more friendly to Gene.

"I want to apologize for the way I've treated you since you and Mom started seeing each other," PJ said. "When I think back at how I manipulated Mom to get what I wanted. Well, I'm surprised you didn't spank me. And Thanksgiving! Well, that was 'behaving badly' at its best!" PJ shook his head at the memory. Gene pulled him in for a hug.

"You saved my mother's life," he said in Gene's ear. "I will always be grateful to you for that. Thank you." PJ pulled away and wiped his eyes. "I understand, now, the love you have for each other. That's how I feel about Meghan." PJ continued. "And without your relationship with my mother, I may not have been born." PJ smiled at Gene through his tears.

"Thank you, son," Gene said. "That's about the finest thing you could say to me."

"Well, you deserve the best and that's my mother!" PJ said, laughing. Gene laughed too.

* * *

Gene

Finally! Alone at last! He waved as Emily and PJ's car left. He loved them but was glad they were gone. He and Kelsey hadn't been alone in forever! Not that they could do anything except hold hands. Doc said no physical activity of any kind for at least three more weeks. Yikes! He couldn't go three days! It would be worth it, though, to have her healthy again. Tonight they would have a quiet dinner and watch the ball drop.

"Hey, baby," Gene said as he walked into his bedroom. They had decided that his room would be the best choice for Kelsey's recovery. It had a king-size bed, flat-screen over the fireplace, bathroom and was close to the kitchen. "What's that?" indicating the wrapped gift on the bed.

"Hey, sweetie," Kelsey said, smiling. "'That' is your Christmas present. Open it! I hope you like it!"

"I'm sure I'll love it. What is it?" he said, tearing the paper off it. "A CD and a DVD…'Persuaded.'" he read. He looked at her questioningly.

"Put the DVD in. You'll see," she said, barely able to contain her excitement.

He put it in the DVD player. Kelsey's face came on the TV screen.

"Hey, Gene. I wanted to do something special for our first Christmas together. Reuniting with you has been such a blessing. I can't begin to tell you how much you mean to me, so I wrote a song." Kelsey paused. "Danny is helping me with harmony." Camera panned to Danny, who waved, smiling like a little boy with a balloon. "And PJ is behind the camera." PJ turned the camera on himself and waved. "I hope you like it…"

Kelsey began to sing:

> I could be persuaded to give my heart to you,
> If you promise not to break it,
> Cause that's so easy to do.

> You could be the answer, to every prayer I've prayed,
> So keep on doing what you do,
> cause I could be persuaded.

> If just one kiss, makes me feel like this,
> I know there's a chance we can make it.
> If you want this dance, offer me your hand,
> Chances are good that I'll take it.

> Cause I could be persuaded, to give my life to you.
> I know it's crazy, maybe we were meant to be,
> Cause I could be persuaded.

> (Musical interlude)

> So keep on doing what you do,
> I could be persuaded.
> I could be persuaded. Yeah, Yeah,
> I could be persuaded.

Gene just stared at the screen, speechless. He looked at Kelsey and back at the screen several times during the song. What a beautiful song! She did this for him? The only song Tracy wrote about him was after they broke up and it wasn't very flattering! When the song was finished, he looked at her with tears in his eyes. "I can't believe you did this for me. Thank you. This is the best gift anyone has ever given me. I love it." He kissed her gently.

"I'm so glad! I was so nervous about it! But Danny kept reassuring me it was going to be fine," Kelsey said. Kelsey told him how much fun it had been recording and collaborating with Danny. "He's a really great producer. He should do more of that."

Right at that moment, Kelsey yawned. "Okay," Gene said, "nap time."

"No, I don't want to. All I ever do, anymore, is sleep!" she protested. She sounded like a whiny toddler.

"C'mon, I'll rub your back until you're asleep. From the look in your eyes, that won't be long!" Kelsey swatted at him but lay on her side. Gene rubbed her back and, in a few minutes, as predicted, was asleep. Gene kissed her shoulder.

* * *

Gene

While Kelsey slept, he looked at the DVD again. He wanted to check something he thought he saw at one point. Wow, it was a good production. PJ did a good job editing. He'd put early pictures of him and Kelsey in as well as some recent ones. He laughed every time he saw their old prom picture!

"You could be the answer…" There it was. That shot of Danny looking at Kelsey. He'd know that look anywhere. He wore it himself whenever he sang with her. Danny was in love with Kelsey. Kelsey told him that she and Danny had gone out a few times during the time Danny had left the band, but they had decided to just be friends. Looks like no one told Danny! Not that he could blame him. Everyone who met Kelsey fell a little in love with her. He's not sure how he feels about his best friend being in love with his girlfriend, though.

CHAPTER SEVENTEEN

A few hours later, Kelsey woke up. They had a late dinner and celebrated the new year. Gene told her he watched the DVD a few more times.

"Didn't PJ do a good job? I'm not sure I wore the right outfit. Did I look all right? I was so self-conscious! Do you really like it?" Kelsey was babbling.

"It's fantastic! In fact, I talked to Danny while you were asleep. He thinks we should have our record company listen to it and release it," he said. Kelsey looked startled.

"No! No!" she shouted. "That's your song. I won't sing it for anyone but you!" Kelsey was getting agitated and started coughing.

"All right, all right, calm down." Gene said. He really wanted to do this for her. She deserved it. She was so talented. "I won't let the record company hear it, I promise. But when you're well, I want to hear it live."

"Deal," she said, clearly relieved.

Their days settled into a routine. Gene and Maria had Kelsey's schedule down pat. Medicine, meals, naps, doctor's appointments. Doc said Gene could take Kelsey outside for some fresh air next week for short periods. PJ and Emily came up on the weekends and they skyped with her too.

He was in the car running some errands for Maria and listening to Kelsey's CD when an old friend called him. Allison Franks. She was pretty big on the Bluegrass charts and had a few country hits as well. He hit the speaker button on his phone. "Hey, Ally! How are you?"

"Hey, Gene," Ally said with a bit of a sexy lilt in her voice. "I'm good, how are you? I thought you were coming to town over Christmas. I expected a call from you."

"Oh yeah, that didn't quite work out the way I had planned." he said. Gene and Ally had a "thing" over the years, getting together when they were both in between relationships. It had helped ease the loneliness for both of them. He hadn't had a chance to tell her about Kelsey.

"What's that your listening to?" she asked. "It's beautiful. Who recorded it? Emmy Lou?"

"No, that's my girlfriend, Kelsey McCoury," he answered proudly. "She wrote it and gave it to me for Christmas." Gene briefly explained how he and Kelsey had reconnected in August, her recent illness and that they were now living together. He left out the part about Emily and James. That was nobody's business. He and Emily had agreed to keep their relationship private.

"Oh…girlfriend," Allison said, disappointed. "Well, sounds like it will be a big hit for her."

"No…she's adamant about keeping the song private. She won't let me play it for the record company," he said as he pulled into the grocery store parking lot. "Last time we spoke, you told me you were getting married," he said changing the subject.

"Yeah well, that didn't work out the way *I* planned!" she said, laughing. "Could I hear the song again?"

"Sure," Gene said. He wanted the whole world to hear this song.

"It's absolutely beautiful, Gene. You can hear the love in her voice," Allison said as the song ended.

"Thanks," Gene said, smiling. "I'm really proud of her."

"Could you e-mail it to me? I'd love to try my hand at it," Allison said. "Maybe Kelsey would let me record it."

Wouldn't that be something? Kelsey would be a bona fide songwriter!

"Kelsey made me promise not to play it for the record company," Gene said. "But she didn't say anything about anyone else." Gene knew he was splitting hairs, but he wanted Kelsey's song to be heard.

"I'll e-mail it this afternoon, and we'll talk in a few days," he said.

A few days later, Allison called, begging to record the song. She hadn't had a hit in a while and knew this song was her ticket back to the top of the charts. She e-mailed Gene her rendition, complete with fiddles, and mandolins. He liked it. He told Allison to come up this weekend and they could both work on getting permission from Kelsey. Emily was coming. She was a *huge* fan of Ally's. First, though, he had to tell Kelsey about his relationship with Allison.

"Hey, baby," Gene said as he walked into the living room. His heart did the familiar flip whenever he saw her. "Can I talk to you?" Kelsey was sitting in front of the big picture window that had a beautiful view of a snow-capped mountain. Her cough was almost gone. Conrad was supposed to call this afternoon, after checking her most recent x-ray, with an update.

"Of course, what's up?" she asked. Just then her phone rang. Kelsey grabbed it. "Hello? Hi, Conrad. Okay...uh huh...uh huh... So I'm cleared for 'physical activity'?" she asked. "Yes? Yes? Here, talk to Gene!" Kelsey jumped up from the couch and handed the phone to Gene. "Keep it short. Come upstairs in five minutes!" Then Kelsey planted a big kiss on Gene's lips.

"Hey! What's going on?" he called after her. "Hey Doc, what's up? Okay...uh huh, that's good news. Oh, that's why she went running up the stairs." Gene started laughing.

"Gene! Get your ass up here! Tell Conrad you'll call him back!" Kelsey yelled.

"Hold on Doc. Hey, Kels, I'm on the phone. Can you wait a minute?" he teased. "Okay, okay, thanks Doc. Come up with Em this weekend. Someone very special is coming."

"Gene." Kelsey whispered in his ear. He turned and saw her standing there in one of his tee shirts. She lifted it up enough to reveal his favorite lace panties of hers.

"Do you really want to keep me waiting?" she said slyly. He dropped the phone on the couch. He quickly picked it up, never taking his eyes off her. "Gotta go, Doc." And he hung up. They raced up the stairs to their bedroom.

Upstairs in their bedroom, all the shades were drawn, and candles were lit. Patsy Cline was coming out of the CD player.

"Wow," he said, looking around. She took his hand and pulled him toward the bed. Very gently, Gene started to make love to her. He was afraid Kelsey wasn't as strong as she thought she was. Wrong! Kelsey flipped him over and started ripping off his jeans. "C'mon, Gene, it's been weeks!" She rubbed his crotch, and instantly he became hard. When she kissed him, she felt the same excitement in herself. They made love with the passion of teenagers.

They spent the whole afternoon making love and planning their future together. They fell asleep wrapped in each other's arms. They still "fit."

CHAPTER EIGHTEEN

The next day, Kelsey wanted to go for a walk down by the lake. It was unseasonably warm for the end of January. Gene bundled her up anyway.

"I look like a snowman!" she said, barely able to move and smiling at his concern.

"You let me know the second you need to come back to the house, okay?" he said. "I don't want you having a relapse."

"Okay, okay, can we go now? I feel like I've been inside forever!" Kelsey was anxious to be outside. They walked down to the lake. It was beautiful. Some of the perennial plants were confused by the weather and starting to sprout.

"Listen, I've invited someone up for the weekend," Gene started, "An old friend, Allison Franks."

"Allison Franks? *The* Allison Franks? Emily is a *huge* fan of hers! She's coming here? We've got to get back to the house and make plans! Does Maria know? I have to help her with the cooking!" Kelsey was babbling excitedly. "We need to call Emily and PJ. Oh, and Danny too!"

"Slow down, slow down," Gene said. "She's coming to meet you."

"Me? Why me?" Kelsey asked, confused.

"She wants to record Persuaded!" Gene said excitedly.

Kelsey looked at him, thunderstruck. "*No!* I told you before, *no!* You promised not to let anyone else hear your song." Kelsey stomped off.

Gene grabbed her arm. "Stop, it wasn't like that. I promised not to let the record company hear the song." Kelsey gave him a look. "Anyway, Allison heard it by accident. She called me and it was playing in the car while I was talking with her," Gene said. "She loved it!"

"I don't care, she can't have it!" Kelsey cried. She started running away from him tearing off her coat and hat as she ran.

"Kelsey! Stop!" Gene cried. He ran after her, pausing only to pick up her outer wear as she threw it off. After a few hundred feet, Kelsey started coughing violently. She sat down on a rock continuing to cough and try to catch her breath.

Gene put the coat around her when he reached her. She was shivering and coughing. "Come on, let's get you home," he said. She huddled against him. "I'm sorry, Gene," Kelsey said, in between coughs. "That was a foolish thing to do."

"It's okay. Can we talk about it at home?" he asked.

Kelsey nodded her head as she continued to cough. They made their way home.

Once he had her settled in bed with a cup of tea (she preferred peach tea with honey), Kelsey covered his hand with hers and started to speak.

"Sweetheart, I know you think you're doing something wonderful for me. Something you think I want," she started. "You've had such great success with the band, and you think that anyone with a little talent wants the same success. And maybe the next song I write, I will want someone to record it. *But not this song!*" Kelsey paused, taking a sip of her tea. "This song is like my children, it has my heart and soul in it. And my love for you. *This is your song.*"

"First of all," Gene answered, "you don't have a 'little' talent, you have a *lot* of talent. And I do want this for you because you deserve it. I am so proud of you." Gene's eyes started to get teary. "Maybe I'm trying to make up for all the years we were apart, those first years after the baby. I don't know." He leaned forward earnestly, holding both her hands in his. "I do know this, that song could have the same meaning for millions of people as it does for you and me. It's *that good*. When I find a song like that, I want to share it. That makes people happy. And me happy. But, the final answer is yours. If you don't give permission, Allison can't record the song. I'll go along with whatever you decide."

* * *

Kelsey

She felt torn. She wanted Gene to be happy. His face just lit up when he talked about the song! Emily and PJ will love the idea of her song being recorded by a major recording artist. Truth is, she's not sure she's ready for all the attention it would bring. She naively thought their relationship would be private.

"Tell you what," Kelsey said, compromising, "I'll listen to her before making a final decision."

Gene's face lit up! "That's all I ask! This is gonna be great! Uh, there is one other thing," Gene said, a little apprehensive. "Allison and I have had an on-and-off 'thing' over the years. A 'friends with benefits' kinda relationship when we were between partners." Kelsey's eyebrow arched up. "Now, we haven't seen each other since before last summer, and it was never anything serious. She told me she was getting married." Gene wanted to reassure Kelsey she had nothing to worry about.

Kelsey set her tea on the nightstand, folded her hands on her lap, and looked at Gene.

"Let me get this straight," she began. "You want a former lover to record a love song that the present love of your life has poured her heart and soul into. Seriously, Gene? What part of your brain thought *that* was a good idea?"

"The only love of my life," he corrected her. "But, now that I hear it out loud, it does sound crazy," Gene said. "But, you're still going to hear her out, right?"

Kelsey leaned back against her pillow and yawned. "I need to sleep." This man was unbelievable!

Chapter Nineteen

* * *

Gene

*H*e was a little nervous about Allison meeting Kelsey. Depending on her mood, Allison could be a wonderful person—polite, friendly, kind. But if she was in one of her "moods," watch out! She could be a real bitch. Allison and Tracy never got along. Tracy insisted Allison was in love with him and jealous of Tracy's talent as a songwriter. He didn't think so. Allison was just as talented in her own right and they had always had an understanding. No commitment, just sex. He decided he was worried about nothing. It would be fine.

* * *

Danny

He was so happy these last few weeks helping take care of Kelsey! He was more in love with her than ever and he knew that was not a good thing, but he couldn't help himself. Just being in her presence was good for him. He started taking better care of himself. Everyone noticed and approved. He liked it.

When he heard Allison was coming to pitch her recording of the song to Kelsey, he was a little worried. In his opinion, Allison was a little bipolar. She could be flying high one minute and a bitch and a half the next. That was great in bed, and he knew that first had. He and Allison got together a time or two when Gene was with Tracy. He had always been stoned. You had to be with Allison. He didn't want her "dark side" to make an appearance this weekend and hurt Kelsey in any way. He'd keep an eye on her and run interference if necessary.

Allison arrived early afternoon on Saturday. Emily and PJ had come up in the morning to help get things ready. They were so excited! Kelsey was still thinking about everything Gene had told her. She supposed relationships were different in his world. Allison was drop dead gorgeous! But also very nice. She even brought a pecan pie for desert! They spent the afternoon getting to know each other and by dinner time, Kelsey was so enamored with her, she wondered why Gene hadn't married her!

Between dinner and desert, Allison played the CD for Kelsey with her rendition of the song. Danny, PJ, and Emily all took seats in the living room. Kelsey was sitting next to Gene on the sofa and he started rubbing Kelsey's back while the song was playing. Kelsey got up to walk around. She couldn't have him touching her while she listened. It didn't feel right. She needed to focus.

* * *

Kelsey

When the song started playing, she almost didn't recognize it. She had recorded it with just an acoustic guitar and mandolin. Allison had added fiddles, pedal steel, and a Dobro. It sounded really, really good. As it played, she could see it. Couples of all ages loving the song, dancing to it, falling in love to it. It was Allison's voice. The song was perfect for her. There was only one decision.

When it finished, there was silence in the room. Everyone held their breath, looking at Kelsey, waiting for her reaction. Kelsey turned to Allison. There was only one thing to say. "It's beautiful," she said. "It's yours." Kelsey went to the kitchen to get dessert.

Allison and Gene looked at each other, surprised. Allison smiled and got up to follow her. She found Kelsey in the kitchen getting things ready for desert.

"Thank you," Allison said. Kelsey just smiled as she arranged the pie, plates and forks on a tray.

"Your welcome," replied Kelsey. She started making coffee as Gene entered the kitchen.

"Allison," Gene said. "Could you give us a minute?"

"Sure," Allison replied. "I was just going to tell Kelsey to buy some new dresses. She'll have a few award shows to attend." Gene smiled and nodded in agreement as Allison left the room. He never took his eyes off Kelsey.

"I felt it," he said to her, watching her make coffee.

"Felt what?" she asked as she poured water in the coffee maker.

"What you were trying to tell me about your feelings for the song," he answered. "Halfway through the song, I saw your face, and I knew you were going to say yes. I felt...sad. I didn't want you to give it away." Gene was as surprised as anyone at his words.

He took Kelsey's hand in his. "Are you sure?"

"Yes, Gene, I'm sure," Kelsey answered. "That song is perfect for Allison's voice. And I could see it, the people, like you said, really loving it. *Are you sure?*"

"Yeah," Gene said, taking her in his arms and kissing her. "Hey, would it be rude if we went to bed early?" he whispered to her as he nibbled on her ear. He knew that drove her crazy.

"Yes, it would," she answered as he kissed her neck. "But I'll let you know when it'll be okay...oh," she groaned. "Stop that," she said, not really wanting him to. They continued to make out and giggle like a couple of teenagers as the coffeepot gurgled.

Allison stood on the other side of the door peeking at them. She had an odd look on her face—a half smile and then a murderous frown. Like she was fighting something inside her.

"Hey, Ally!" Danny called. "C'mon back!" Allison turned, shook her head, and went back to the living room.

When the coffee was ready, Gene and Kelsey came back out to the living room to join everyone for desert. Everyone was talking and laughing. Pretty soon the guitars came out, and everyone jammed and started singing. The beer and liquor flowed as freely as the music.

Kelsey gave Gene a look, and he nodded. She yawned. "I think I'll head up to bed, everyone. It's been a long, exciting day." Gene stretched and agreed. "See everyone in the morning," he said. Once they had left the living room, they smiled and ran up the stairs. Everyone was spending the night. Emily and Allison were sharing the guest room across from Gene's bedroom. PJ and Danny were sleeping in the other guest room on the other side of the house.

While Kelsey waited for Gene to finish up in the bathroom, she lay in their bed thinking how her life was going to change, again! First, she's a school teacher, then the girlfriend of a country star, and now a songwriter! Allison seemed to think Persuaded was going to be huge hit. The money she was talking about was enormous! She had always wanted to put in a recording studio at school. Maybe now she could.

Allison said it would definitely top the bluegrass charts. It may even cross over to the country and pop charts. She had not seen any of the award shows over the years. She was too afraid she would see Gene on camera. Now she would be attending with him. In just six short months, she had reunited with Gene, retired from her teaching position, moved in with him and about to launch a new career as a songwriter! Whew!

"Hey, you," Gene said as he slid under the sheets next to her and taking her in his arms. "What are you thinking about?"

"You," she answered, smiling.

"That's what I like to hear," he said, kissing her.

Chapter Twenty

The next morning, Kelsey got up to make a big breakfast for everyone. Gene was still asleep after she had her shower and finished dressing, so she went to the kitchen to start cooking—pancakes, eggs, bacon and toast, coffee, and juice. Emily had come in the kitchen and was helping her.

"Mom, Allison never came to bed last night," Emily said as she buttered toast. "And it looks like someone slept on the couch."

"What? Oh, that means," She looked at Emily. "Danny?"

"Or PJ," Emily said mischievously.

"It better not be PJ!" Kelsey said. They both laughed. Then Kelsey looked turned serious. She didn't like the idea of Allison sleeping with either one of them. At that moment, Danny walked into the room, looking like the walking dead. Looks like we have a winner!

"Rough night?" Kelsey asked, turning her back on him and walking to the stove. She started banging pots and pans around. Why should she be upset if Danny had slept with Allison?

"Must have been," he answered as he poured himself a cup of coffee. "'Cause I don't remember." Allison walked in looking as fresh as a daisy and gave Danny a big smile. He smiled back, sheepishly.

"Good morning, everyone! Breakfast smells heavenly!" Allison said.

Kelsey shooed everyone to the table and served breakfast. By that time, PJ and Gene had made their way to the dining room. Kelsey was polite and friendly to Allison but treated Danny with indifference. She answered his questions with one-word answers and mostly tried to ignore him.

* * *

Danny

He hadn't planned on sleeping with Allison, but she had a strange look on her face when she came from the kitchen after Kelsey gave her permission to record the song. He had poured himself a drink. Kelsey didn't allow pot or drugs in the house. A little while after Gene and Kelsey went to bed he found Allison in the hallway outside their room. Just staring at the door. Time to run interference. He had gotten so drunk! But it worked. He had kept her away from them. The sex wasn't bad either.

But why was Kelsey acting like she was mad at him? She acted like he committed a crime! Maybe he should tell her about the sacrifice he had made! Was she jealous? No, they were only friends. That's the way she wanted it. She had made that clear. Oh, his head hurt! He couldn't think about anything right now.

* * *

Gene

He looked at Danny and then Allison while he sipped his coffee. Looks like they got together last night. Danny was hungover and Allison had the cat-who-swallowed-the-canary kind of smile on her face. That was fine with him. But what was Kelsey's problem? She sure was acting funny. Nice to Allison but treating Danny like he's a leper! Women!

Around 11:00 AM, everyone started getting ready to go home. Emily and PJ left together. A car came from the record company to pick up Allison. Allison tried to get Danny to come back to Nashville with her, but he put her off making up an excuse. Kelsey frowned, watching from the window as they kissed goodbye. Why is their relationship bothering her?

"I think I'll try to make twelve o'clock mass at St. Marks," Kelsey said to Gene, turning from the window.

"Sounds good," he answered. "I'll go with you."

At St. Marks, Kelsey prayed for Danny. This morning was the first time she had seen him hung over since she started seeing Gene. She hoped it was just a slip up. Then she prayed for herself. Later that week, she had a board meeting with her brothers and sisters for the school. She intends to address her relationship with Gene, their role in it, and the future care of their parents after they finished with school business.

CHAPTER TWENTY-ONE

"*O*kay, come to order," Jerry said, banging a gavel. He was a little dramatic with that thing. They all looked at the agenda for the meeting and settled down to business.

"What's this item, recording studio?" asked Robert.

"I want to put one in," said Kelsey.

"There's no money for that, Kels, you know that.," Robert said.

"I just sold a song. I'll fund it," she answered. She waited for their reaction.

Everyone started speaking at once. "Sold a song? What song? When…how…who?"

Kelsey told them the story of Persuaded and how Allison Franks was going to record it. *And* the amount of money she was paying for the privilege. It would more than cover a recording studio for the school. The rest she would put in the scholarship fund.

"Wow, that is so cool, Kels!" cried Toni. "When will we hear it on the radio?"

"Probably a few weeks. Gene and I will be heading to Nashville to do some preliminary promotion for it. I'll let you know," she answered.

"Speaking of Gene," she started, standing up, "there's something I want to talk to all of you about." Kelsey cleared her throat. "I know what happened when I lost James and the first year after." She looked around the table at Jerry, Robert, Sandy, and finally, her mother. They all looked down. Her mother started crying softly. Her younger siblings looked confused. She explained to them what had happened to her. They had been too young at the time to remember and were shocked at what she told them.

"We thought we were doing what was best, at the time," her mother said, wiping her eyes and blowing her nose.

"By lying to me?" Kelsey cried. "Keeping Gene away when I kept asking for him? Taking his letters and not telling me about his phone calls? You thought that was best for me? Mom, did you know I thought about suicide more than once that first year? I developed trust issues where men were concerned. It shaped my whole being! And not in a good way!"

"But you met Peter and went on to have a happy life!" her mother answered.

"I did, but it wasn't easy getting to that point. And it should have been *my* choice, *my* decision. And I probably would have made it! Mom, can you imagine what it feels like to know you're own family doesn't trust your judgment? You raised me, for God's sake! Why wouldn't you trust me? And you three!" Kelsey said, looking at Jerry, Robert, and Sandy. "How could you? You're my brothers and sister!"

"We didn't have much of a choice, Dad made us.," Sandy said. She was always a wimp when it came to their father. Jerry and Robert stayed silent.

"Oh please! You were all adults at the time! Old enough to know the difference between right and wrong! Toni was the only one with any balls! She let Gene know what had happened. When he got to the hospital, he was able to hold the baby and say goodbye. He was also in my room with me, like he promised." Kelsey looked pointedly at her mother, who was still crying. The others all looked at each other. They didn't know Gene had made it to the hospital. By this time, Kelsey was crying.

"We're sorry, Kels," Robert said. "I don't know what else to say. Dad was very convincing at the time that it was the right thing to do." The others nodded in agreement.

"Well, sorry won't cut it right now!" Kelsey cried. "Oh, I'm so mad at all of you!" Kelsey continued to cry. "This was my life you were playing with!" Kelsey's tears turned to coughing. Toni rushed over to her. "That's enough! This meeting is over!" Jerry half-heartedly banged his gavel. They all left the room. Her younger siblings hugging her before they left. Her mother stayed.

After everyone left, her mother said, quietly, "I saved all of his letters." Kelsey stopped coughing and looked at her.

"What?" Kelsey asked, holding her chest in pain.

"Gene's letters, I saved them. He wrote every week for over a year."

"You did?" she asked. Her mother nodded and pulled a stack of letters out of her handbag and handed them to her. Toni had warned her that Kelsey was going to talk about Gene at the meeting.

"I didn't agree with your father's plan," her mother said. "But he was my husband. Things were different in those days. I had to believe he had your best interest in his heart." She heaved a big sigh. "I don't know why I saved them. Seemed to be the right thing to do at the time."

"Oh, Mom, Mommy, thank you." Kelsey took the letters and got up to hug her.

"And don't worry about your father and me," she said, hugging her back. "Toni has been a big help since your illness and will be taking over all your responsibilities where we are concerned. Whatever she can't handle, one of your brothers and sisters will take care of it. Go, live your life. I love you, baby." Kelsey looked at her mother with tears in her eyes and then looked at the letters. All of a sudden, she felt very blessed.

Kelsey came home from the meeting totally drained and took a long nap. Afterward, at dinner she told Gene about it and showed him his letters. Gene knew Kelsey's mom had always liked him. Their mothers had been best friends when they were growing up. After the baby, it was a real strain on their relationship. He had always felt guilty about that. Both women were married to very strong men, and in those days, you didn't go against your husband's wishes. Their friendship did not survive.

Chapter Twenty-Two

* * *

Kelsey

*S*he shut herself up in her room after dinner to read Gene's letters. They had decided to turn the guest room across from Gene's room into a room for her for when she needed her own space. Besides a bed, she had her own walk in closet, bathroom, and sitting area. Having a man to sleep with is great, but she loved having her own closet and bathroom!

She spread the letters out on the bed and looked at the dates on the postmarks. Wow, he wrote faithfully every week for more than a year. The postmarks were from all over the country. She sucked in her breath as she opened the first letter. "My Darling Kelsey," it began. By the time she got to the end, she was crying, remembering what she was going through as she read Gene's words. She's not sure she can read the rest. At least not tonight. She needs to talk to Gene. She found him in his recording studio.

"Hey," Kelsey said to him as she walked in. "Got a minute?"

"As many as you want," he answered as he adjusted one of the dials on the board and took off his headphones. "What's up?"

"I read your first letter," she said, wiping her eyes. He looked up at her with concern. "I'm afraid to read the rest. I couldn't get through the first one without crying and remembering."

"You know, there's no rush," he said. "It's been thirty-six years. If it's that upsetting, you should take your time." he paused, hesitating. "Would it…would it help if I were with you when you read them?" Gene wasn't sure what to say. He had poured his heart and soul into every one of those letters. He wasn't sure he could read them again.

"Probably…but I can tell by the look on your face that you don't want to," she said. This was tough on him too. "You're right. There's no rush. I don't have to read them all tonight." Kelsey walked over to him and kissed him. "I'm sorry," she whispered. Gene hugged her back. She vowed to herself that she would read them herself and not hurt him again.

They were scheduled to go to Nashville on Valentine's Day weekend for the recording session of Persuaded. Allison and The record company wanted Kelsey to sing back up on the single. Kelsey was very excited. She had started coughing a little but wasn't concerned. Conrad told her to get plenty of rest and drink lots of water. She should be fine.

They flew in with Danny on a Thursday and stayed at the Opryland Hotel. Gene took her all over the city the next day showing her his favorite places. They found a great antique store that had a lot of music merchandise. Gene was looking at guitars while Kelsey wandered around. The store manager saw her looking at the jewelry and they started talking. Kelsey had always wanted a ring and earrings of her birthstone, emerald. The manager showed her what they had in the showcase. Kelsey didn't know it, but Gene had arranged coming here in advance and the store manager was actually helping Kelsey pick out her engagement ring! Kelsey saw a pair of earrings that she fell in love with too. Ever frugal, she couldn't see spending $500 on them! She found two rings she liked also. But she couldn't bring herself to spend that much money on jewelry. Gene knew she wouldn't spend money on herself. He just needed a little help with what to get her.

On Saturday, Gene had a surprise for her. The session with Allison was scheduled for around 4:00 PM. Gene arranged for some musician friends to join them in the morning so Kelsey could have the experience of recording some of her favorite songs in a real recording studio.

They were at the studio, looking over songs, deciding what to record when Kelsey looked up and saw her absolute favorite bluegrass artist walk through the door. Her mouth dropped to the floor. Cody Rogers!

"Hey, Gene! How are you?" Cody said, shaking Gene's hand.

"Hey, Cody, thanks for coming!" Gene answered. Kelsey couldn't move.

"This must be Kelsey," Cody said, taking her hand in his. Kelsey was speechless. The only man she had ever truly lusted after was Cody Rogers. He rivaled Bradley Cooper when it came to handsome. Sure, she loved Pete and Gene, but for just mind blowing sex, Cody was *it!* She and Pete had gone to many of his concerts over the years. Pete used to tease her all the time about him. All Cody had to do was crook his little finger, and she would go running. And now he was standing in front of her, holding her hand and smiling at her.

"I'm really looking forward to working with you today," Cody said, still holding her hand.

"You're Cody Rogers," she said, stupidly, staring at him.

"Yes, I am," he laughed, still holding her hand, looking at her with those heavenly green eyes of his. "Nice to meet you."

Kelsey looked at Gene, who was smiling, "Surprise!" he said. She would kill him later. Right now, she needed to get herself together. Kelsey stood up and shook Cody's hand. "It's an honor, Cody. My late husband and I have been fans for many years." Kelsey stared into his eyes and smiled nervously. They were captivating.

"The honor is mine," he said, covering her hand with his and caressing it. "I've heard your song. It's beautiful. You can count me as one of your fans." Kelsey blushed, watching him caress her hand. She didn't want him to stop.

"Now, what would you like to sing today?" he asked. Gene smiled. Kelsey was so happy. He noticed that Cody was still holding Kelsey's hand. He shook his head as he smiled at them. Everyone fell in love with Kelsey as soon as they met her.

Chapter Twenty-Three

* * *

Kelsey

*W*hat a day! Singing and recording in a real recording studio, with professional musicians and meeting Cody Rogers! She could not believe she had actually met him! He held her hand! Loved her song! This was crazy! How did she get here?

They rehearsed Persuaded for when Allison came later. Then they recorded some of Kelsey's favorite songs. She sang a few by herself, a duet with Cody, Jimmy, and she sang with Gene also. They were all sitting in the engineer's booth, listening to the recordings when Allison got there. By this time, Kelsey was much more comfortable with Cody. They had hung out all afternoon. He was just as nice off stage as he was on. They were becoming great friends. Allison came in around 4:30 PM looking pissed.

"What's everyone sitting around for? This is my money your wasting!" Allison screamed. "What are you listening to? Sounds like crap! Let's get to work, I don't have all day!" She stomped out of the room into the studio. They all looked at each other in bewilderment. What the hell?

"Well, everyone," Danny said, "Hurricane Allison has made landfall!" They all got up and followed her into the studio, chuckling.

* * *

Kelsey

What the hell was that? She had never seen Allison like that. Then again they had just met a few weeks ago. No one seemed disturbed by her attitude. She had a lot to learn about big recording stars!

They all took their places and started running through the song. Kelsey and Gene shared a mic. Nothing seemed to go right, according to Allison. She was nice one minute and would bit your head off the next. Mostly, she bit off Gene's head. Kelsey tried to stay out of her line of fire. She didn't think Allison was in the right frame of mind to sing the song, but it wasn't her call to make. Kelsey hated the way Allison was treating Gene. Finally after about two hours of Allison harassing everyone, Kelsey decided she needed a break and went out in the hallway. She came back in through the engineer's booth. George, the engineer, didn't know she was behind him. He had Allison's mic on and they were arguing.

"But, Ally, I don't understand what you want," George was saying.

"I want that slut out of here!" Allison shouted. The musicians just looked down at their music, pretending not to hear. "So what if she wrote the song? I don't want her here! I don't care what the record company wants!" Allison was near hysterical. Kelsey stayed by the door. No one could see her. She went numb. She blinked back tears.

"Ally…calm down," Gene said. "We'll work this out."

"You shut up! I can't stand looking at the two of you!" Allison screamed at him. "Making goo-goo eyes at each other and holding hands. Are you kidding me?"

"What are you talking about, Al?" Gene asked, surprised.

"I'm talking about us, Gene!" Allison cried, near tears. "You were supposed to come at Christmas time! Fall in love with me! I've been waiting and waiting for you Gene!" Gene was so shocked he couldn't speak. He had always been brutally honest with Allison about their relationship.

At this point, the guys got up and beat a hasty exit out the door. Danny went through the booth to tell George they would be out in the hall. Then he saw Kelsey standing by the door.

"Oh shit!" he said, looking at the door. George turned around. "Uh-oh."

Kelsey ran into the hallway and slammed right into Cody.

"Hey, where's the fire!" Cody said, laughing. Then he saw the tears in Kelsey's eyes and quickly figured out that she had heard Allison's rant. She struggled to get away from him.

"No!" he said, holding on to her. "You are not running away! Allison and Gene will iron this out. They always do. You run and she wins!" He pulled her close, saying in her ear, "*And no tears. You're stronger than that.*"

Kelsey stopped struggling and looked at him. He was right. They were all adults. This was teenage stuff. She was done being intimidated by Allison Franks. Kelsey stood up tall, straightened her blouse and put on her jacket. She looked Cody right in the eye.

"I think we're done here," she told him. "Would you mind taking me back to the hotel, Cody? I'd like to rest before dinner, and Gene probably has his hands full."

"I'd be mighty proud to, ma'am." Cody laughed and turned to the rest of the band. "We're done here, guys, thanks for your time." The guys nodded, thanked Kelsey, and walked toward the door.

By that time, Danny had joined them. "I'll take her, Cody," he said, taking Kelsey's elbow, "I'm going that way." He steered Kelsey toward the door. Cody stood there, a little dumbfounded, then shook his head, and laughed. "See you guys later," he called. Kelsey turned and waved.

"That was a little rude, Danny," Kelsey said.

"I didn't like the way he looked at you all afternoon," Danny said. "And I didn't like the way you looked back!" Danny was clearly pissed off as they got into a cab.

"Seriously, Danny?" Kelsey asked, cocking her head to one side.

Danny's anger melted as she smiled at him. "Sorry," he said, "I'll apologize to Cody later. Are you okay?" He put his arm around her.

"I'm fine. I feel bad for Gene, though," she said as the cab sped toward their hotel. "Allison is probably ripping him a new one. Did you know she was in love with him?"

Danny look away from her. "She's not in love with him. Allison just wants what she can't have." They pulled up to the hotel, paid the driver, and walked to their rooms.

"Is that why you slept with her at the house? To keep her away from Gene?" she asked, stopping outside her door.

Danny looked down and shook his head. He couldn't risk looking at her. She would guess the truth. "I'll see you at dinner," he said and went to his room.

Kelsey watched him leave, not knowing what to think. She texted Gene that she had made it back to the hotel and would wait for him there. She had started coughing, so she took some of the medicine Conrad had given her and lay down until it was time to get ready for dinner.

CHAPTER TWENTY-FOUR

A little while later, Gene crawled into bed with her.

"Hey, sweetie," Kelsey said, snuggling next to him. She could tell he was exhausted. He and Allison had argued about their relationship and Kelsey for another half an hour. Gene had no idea Allison had this whole fantasy built up in her mind about them being together. He managed to calm her down and set her straight. They had parted on good terms, he thought. He's not sure about anything when it comes to her anymore.

"Hey, beautiful," Gene answered as he held her. He was so blessed. All the stress of the afternoon melted away as he held her. They both fell back to sleep for a few minutes. Later on they joined Danny and Cody at the Wildhorse Saloon for dinner. It had great food and even better music.

* * *

Kelsey

Poor Gene! She could only imagine what he went through with Allison after they left the studio. She didn't ask the details. He told her they had talked everything out and Allison understood that the relationship they had had was over. Nothing was going to change that. Allison told him she understood. Then he asked her about the record. Allison told her they had cut it the day before. The record company had changed the date at the last minute, and she hadn't had time to tell him. Or so she said.

Wow, that girl knew all kinds of ways to humiliate and embarrass her. They had been in town since Thursday. Well, it was done and she had had a great day in the studio, recording, meeting Cody and the others. It would always be a great memory in spite of how it ended. She would have to be on her guard any time she saw Allison from now on.

"So," Cody said after they finished eating, "Danny says the story of how you two met is a Lifetime movie. Could I hear it?"

"Well," Gene began, "I was ten and she was eight…"

"I'm going to stop you right there, honey," said Kelsey. Turning to Danny, she said, "Danny, would you like to dance?"

"Sure!" Danny answered, getting up.

"Cody," Kelsey said, turning toward him and squeezing Gene's hand, "Gene loves to tell this story so I'll let him do it. This music is too good." She grabbed Danny's hand and they headed for the dance floor.

Gene just sat there smiling and watching them.

"So," Cody prompted, "You were ten and she was eight… continue."

"Oh, right," Gene said, coming back. Gene recounted the story, including losing the baby, finding out he had a daughter, and finding Kelsey again. Cody was good friend. He had lost his wife last year to cancer. Gene had helped him through that and knew he could trust him.

* * *

Cody

He sat there listening to Gene tell the story of his and Kelsey's relationship and knew there was a song in there somewhere. He hoped it would come to him. As Gene talked, he thought of Kathy, his late wife. Their story wasn't as dramatic, but he had loved her for more than thirty years and missed her terribly. He looked at the dance floor at Kelsey and Danny. He had been captivated by Kelsey the moment he saw her in the recording studio. The last woman to have that effect on him *was* Kathy. When Gene had asked him last week about coming by the studio today, he resisted. He was still in the "hibernating" stage of his grief. But Gene kept at him, telling him he needed to get back in the studio, Kelsey was such a big fan, they really needed his help, etc., etc. So he came. He was glad he had. Kelsey McCoury sure was something. Beautiful, talented, bubbly, full of life. He looked forward to their friendship. Anything more than that, he knew he would be third in line behind Danny from the way he was looking at her.

A little while later, Kelsey came back to the table. She took Cody's hand and dragged him onto the dance floor.

"Some chick cut in and stole Danny," she said. "You're up, Cody."

"What about Gene?" he asked as they started to two-step.

"He only slow dances with me," Kelsey answered, shrugging.

"Lucky him," Cody muttered under his breath.

"What?" Kelsey asked.

"Nothing," Cody answered as he swung her around and laughed at himself.

Two songs later, "Crazy" started playing, and sure enough, Gene popped up to cut in on them. "Thanks, Cody," Gene said.

"Anytime, buddy," Cody answered as he returned to the table. He sat down next to Danny. They watched Kelsey and Gene dance from their table.

"I'm sorry, Cody, about that remark I made this afternoon," Danny said.

"No worries, Dan," Cody answered. "I think I know how you feel." Cody nodded his head toward Gene and Kelsey and then looked over at Danny. They smiled at each other, understanding.

As they danced Gene took a small box out of his pocket.

"I've got a Valentine's present for you." He handed it to her. Kelsey's face lit up. "Genie! You didn't have to do that!" she squealed. "But I'm glad you did!" She tore opened the wrapping and opened it. Inside were the emerald earrings she had seen at the antique store yesterday!

"Oh my!" she exclaimed. "They're beautiful! But they're so expensive, Gene! Oh, but I love them!" She hugged and kissed him right on the dance floor. The couples around them laughed and clapped. "Nice job, guy!" someone yelled. They both laughed. Kelsey didn't know it but there was a matching engagement ring in the not too distant future.

Gene and Kelsey started kissing, and he danced her into a dark corner of the club behind a big artificial plant. "Hey, I have something back at the hotel that would look great with these earrings," she whispered in between kisses. "What's that?" he asked playfully. "My cream silk robe," she whispered, kissing him and running her hand over his crotch. "With matching lace panties." He grabbed her hand. "I'm not going to make it back to the hotel." he said to her. Gene led her down the hall way to where the dressing rooms were located. He opened one, peeked inside and led her in. He turned and put a hanger on the door handle before closing and locking it. Gene pushed Kelsey up against the wall, pressing his erection against her.

"Stop, Gene!" Kelsey gasped. "We can't do it here! Someone will walk in on us." She tried to stop his hands that were already starting to undress her. This was definitely outside her comfort zone.

"That's what the hanger is for." he said, smiling at her and continued to undress her. Kelsey was pretty conservative when it came to sex. But then, with Gene, every day was a new adventure. Okay, she could play along.

Kelsey pulled the condom out of his front pocket and pushed him on the couch. Tossing the package at him, she said, "Be a good boy and open this." While he fumbled with the condom package, she shimmed out of her jeans. He glanced up and saw she was already wearing the lace panties. He ran his finger under the elastic and looked at her.

"I was a Girl Scout, remember." She said. "I always try to be prepared." He laughed. She climbed on top of him.

"Wanna go for a ride?" Gene asked. She nodded as she settled herself and they started moving in rhythm with each other. They didn't take their eyes off of each other. Gene could not believe this was the Kelsey he grew up and fell in love with.

"Oh Gene... That's so good, baby... Harder..." Kelsey whispered in his ear. The talk got "dirtier" and the sex more intense. Gene had a hard time keeping up with her. When they finished, they just leaned against each other, panting, trying to catch their breath.

"Who are you and what have you done with my Kelsey?" He asked, panting. Kelsey smiled as she caught her breath and kissed his forehead. She climbed off of him and started dressing. As she was looking in the mirror, putting in her new earrings, Gene came up behind her and put his arms around her waist, hugging her to him.

"Where did a nice Catholic girl like you learn to talk like that?" he asked, kissing the side of her head.

Kelsey smiled, her half smile and said, "You don't know everything about me."

"Let's go back to the hotel." Gene said. "I want to learn 'everything.'" They went back out to the club and made their excuses to Danny and Cody and headed back to the hotel. Danny and Cody enjoyed the rest of the evening with Danny's dance partner and her friend.

CHAPTER TWENTY-FIVE

*T*hey left for home the next day. Persuaded was released the first week of March. It premiered at number twenty-five! This was unheard of! People were downloading it from iTunes at an unprecedented rate! Kelsey was at school helping PJ when they heard it come on the radio.

"Ms. Kelsey, is that your song?" Carol asked. Carol was one on her former and now PJ's student.

"Yes, it is Carol," she answered, smiling. Just then her phone vibrated. It was Gene.

"Do you hear it?" he said excitedly. "Do you hear it?"

"Yes, Gene, I hear it!" She laughed at him. He was more excited than she was! By this time, PJ had piped it in to the PA system, and the whole school was listening. It was glorious!

Later that night, after dinner, Gene went looking for Kelsey. He found her sitting in her favorite place, in front of the big picture window with a view of the mountains, working on her laptop. He stopped to study her. Gene loved the way her bottom lip stuck out when she was concentrating. His heart did the usual flip. Gene checked his pocket for the ring box and let out a big breath. All right, it was now or never!

"Hey," he said, sliding onto the couch next to her. "What are you working on?"

"A story idea I have," she answered. He read what she had written over her shoulder.

"Is that about us?" he asked.

"A little," she answered. "It's not something I'm looking to pub-lish. I'm just doing it for fun."

He looked at her with a raised eyebrow. "You write songs, I write stories," she said, shrugging.

"Okay," Gene said, sitting up, "I have a question for you and I need your undivided attention."

"You got it," she said, closing her laptop. "Shoot."

Gene took the ring box out of his pocket, looked at Kelsey, and got down on one knee. Kelsey sucked in her breath in surprise.

"Kelsey, I did this once before and you said 'yes.' I'm hoping you say 'yes' again." Gene took the ring out of the box and held it out to her. It was the antique emerald ring she had seen in Nashville. The one that matched her ear rings. Her eyes started tearing up.

"Oh, Gene! It's beautiful!" Kelsey exclaimed.

"Kelsey, I have loved you practically my whole life. I wake up every morning with this indescribable happiness that I have never felt before. I want that feeling for the rest of my days. Will you marry me?" He looked at her, hopefully.

"Oh, Gene…yes…yes… Yes!" Kelsey watched as he slipped the ring on her finger and kissed her hand. She threw herself in to his arms, and they both fell over on the floor, laughing.

CHAPTER TWENTY-SIX

The band had a few dates between the end of February and the opening of the Bluebird Cafe which officially opened on March 15th. Kelsey grumbled a bit about all the travel time, but she was always ready to go when Gene needed her. The club offered appetizers, snacks, drinks, dancing, and live entertainment. Declan and Gene produced the shows that showcased new singer and songwriters several days a week and for corporate events. They were even sponsoring a songwriting event for local high schools. That had been Kelsey's idea. Her mantra was get the kids involved and their parents will come. A satisfied customer was still the best advertising. When Gene left Declan in charge of the negotiations, Declan had made sure Kelsey became part of the team. They had several talks between Thanksgiving and before they left for Nashville last Christmas about marketing the shows. Declan loved all her ideas. He knew he was taking a chance, committing her without even asking. But it paid off. She loved being part of it all. Declan and Karen were closing on their Nashville home next month. He hoped his father and Kelsey would follow them soon. Right now, she worked a lot of the details out with the club manager by Skype and text in between the FyreByrd's dates, helping PJ out at school and getting her house ready to sell.

The first *celebrity* showcase was going to be The FyreByrds with Kelsey as the featured songwriter. Persuaded was tearing up the Bluegrass charts and recently broke through the country charts and was climbing.

The show was going to be FyreByrds music with Gene and Kelsey talking about their relationship in between songs. Cody,

Danny, and the rest of the band would also be there. Kelsey had written two more songs they would include, and Allison was going to sing Persuaded to close the show.

Gene and Kelsey arrived on Tuesday of that last week in April. The show was on Saturday night. The week was a whirlwind of rehearsals, interviews, shopping for clothes for the show, working out the details. Gene was a nervous wreck all week. Allison was scheduled for rehearsal Saturday morning and to close the show Saturday night. He hoped there wouldn't be a repeat of February's visit to Nashville. You just never knew with Allison.

Kelsey was exhausted. And it was only Friday. She had started coughing a few weeks ago. Conrad had given her some cough syrup. This week it had started getting worse. Gene was so preoccupied that he didn't notice. Kelsey should own stock in the cough syrup company. He really wanted the show to go well for her and the song. He had been snapping at her about stupid stuff all week and then he'd apologize. Kelsey suspected it had to do with Allison. Every time his phone rang, it was her with a new idea or demand for the show. They just had to get through a few more days.

Saturday morning Kelsey woke up to hear Gene in the other room, arguing with Allison on the phone. "What do you mean, you won't be at rehearsal today?" Gene asked, clearly pissed off. "We set this up weeks ago, Ally!"

She listened from the doorway. Damn that woman. She coughed. Okay, time for a hot shower and cough medicine. Kelsey could help Gene by doing her best tonight. When she was dressed and ready for the day, she came out of the bedroom of their suite for breakfast. Gene waved "good morning" to her because, of course, he was on the phone. Kelsey sighed, looking at her schedule for the day. Wow, so many interviews. And they all asked the same questions. If she had to tell the story of the first time they met one more time, she thought she might scream. She wished there was a way to do them all at once.

Cody and Danny arrived to picked her up to take her to the radio interviews. She waved goodbye to Gene, but he was on the phone. At the second radio station, she started losing her voice.

"Hey, are you all right?" Danny asked.

"I'm fine," she said, whispering. "I've just been doing a lot of interviews this week."

"I've noticed some coughing too," Cody said. Danny and Kelsey looked at each other.

"Something you two want to tell me?" he asked. Cody was more than a little concerned.

"No." Kelsey coughed. "Yes." Danny said at the same time.

"Kelsey had a bad case of pneumonia a while back." Danny said. Kelsey glared at him. "Are you sure you're all right?" he said to Kelsey.

"I'll be fine," she whispered. She wasn't very convincing. Then she coughed. A real, *painful*, chest hurting cough. Cody made an executive decision. "We're going to my doctor" he announced. Kelsey started to protest. Cody overruled her and took her to his doctor's office.

Dr. Adam Melendez has been Cody's doctor for a few years now. He worked out of a local hospital and had several country music stars as patients. He was also very handsome. The quintessential tall, dark and handsome. He examined Kelsey, looked down her throat and listened to her lungs.

"How long since the pneumonia?" he asked.

"Let's see," she answered. "Beginning of January. My doctor cleared me in the beginning of February to resume all my normal activities."

"What have you been doing since then?" he asked, leaning against the counter in the exam room.

"Well, we've been to Nashville three times. Out on the road with the band." she answered, "And when we're home, I help my son at school and get my house ready to sell." Kelsey averted her eyes then and blushed a little. She didn't want to tell Dr. Melendez *everything* she was doing. Her sex life had *never* been this good, even when she was married.

Dr. Melendez smiled, a little confused by Kelsey's blushing. "That doesn't sound normal, it sounds busy." he said. "Are you eating right? Getting proper rest?" he asked. "I'm sure your doctor told you not to over due it."

"Busy is my normal, Doc. What are you trying to tell me?" Kelsey asked. It's too bad Emily was seeing Conrad. Dr. Adam Melendez was a serious looker!

"I'm trying to tell you that you are headed for a relapse." He said, looking her in the eye. "I can hear some crackling in your lungs, and your glands are swollen." He paused. "I don't think you should do the show tonight."

"*That* is not an option." she said sternly, looking directly back at him. "Gene and Declan have been planning this for weeks, I won't let them down." She stopped, thinking. "How about a compromise?" she said. "I'll keep my mouth shut the rest of the day and come in for an x-ray and blood work tomorrow. That way I can sing tonight." She smiled sweetly at him and stroked his arm. "Deal?"

Adam Melendez was a sucker for a sweet smile. He smiled back and reluctantly agreed. "But I get a seat down front, so I can keep an eye on you." He tried to be stern.

He failed. Kelsey threw her arms around him and said, "You got it! Thank you!"

"Excuse me?" he said.

"You got it! Thank you!" Kelsey whispered.

CHAPTER TWENTY-SEVEN

*A*fter hearing what the doctor said, Cody took charge of the situation. He arranged for the rest of the interviews to be done during the showcase since Gene and Kelsey would be talking about their relationship in between songs. The radio stations were all agreeable since they were getting to see the show in addition to the interview. That will be great promotion for the club on their show Monday morning. Cody even invited the two stations they had already done. Kelsey went back to the hotel with strict orders to rest and drink plenty of fluids. Kelsey had her own strict orders for Cody and Danny—they were *not* to tell Gene anything. Tomorrow would be soon enough. The show would be over, and they could both rest. They both reluctantly agreed.

* * *

Danny

He did not like keeping this from Gene. He agreed with the doctor. They could rearrange the show. Allison could sing a few of the songs. Besides the coughing, Kelsey looked very pale. He had tried to convince her, but she was determined to do this for Gene, not let him down. All he could do was be there for her.

Back at the hotel, Kelsey couldn't rest. She was too excited. She was also getting nervous. Most of the audience would be music critics and reporters. They could make or break the club. She kept her promise though and didn't talk. Thank God for texting! Kelsey texted Emily about what was happening. *Conrad* texted her back and scolded her. So much for mother and daughter secrets! He scolded her again a little while later after he heard the details from Dr. Melendez. One of the hotel staff, Collin, checked on her. He brought her tea, water, anything he thought she needed. Kelsey was so grateful for his kindness she gave him a couple of tickets to the show. His mother was a big fan. She checked her outfit, repressed her pants, again.

Kelsey texted Gene but all she got back was, "Busy, talk later." Kelsey really wished she could talk to him. They hadn't had any time alone all week. She missed him, but she knew it was better that he didn't know the full extent of her illness. Not yet anyway. Finally, she put out the Do Not Disturb sign, set her alarm, and lay down. The next thing she knew, the alarm was singing, and it was time to get up. Wow, how could a person sleep for thirty minutes and wake up exhausted? Chloe, from the club, was coming over to help her with her hair and makeup. She steamed up the bathroom to help clear her lungs. Kelsey looked at the instructions for the pills Dr. Melendez had sent over. "May cause drowsiness." Well, she couldn't take one now. She'll take it tonight after the show. It'll be fine.

Two hours later, Chloe had worked her magic and Kelsey was ready to go. Cody knocked on the door, ready to escort her to the club. Kelsey answered it.

"Hey, Cody," she said smiling at him. God, he's gorgeous, she thought. "C'mon in."

"Wow! You look like a million dollars!" Cody said. He couldn't take his eyes off her.

"It's all Chloe," she said, modestly, grabbing her jacket and purse. "Let's go."

They arrived in time for sound check. Kelsey warmed up her voice. She sounded good. She gave Cody and Danny a thumbs up. Cody nodded his approval from the back of the club.

Gene walked over and kissed her cheek. "You look beautiful, baby," he said as his phone rang. He glanced at it and but didn't answer. Kelsey thought that was odd given that the phone had been attached to his ear all week. "I have to talk to you about something."

That didn't sound good. "Sure, sweetie," Kelsey answered. "You look beautiful too," she said, trying to make him smile. He gave her a weak smile. Uh-oh. Something was definitely wrong. They went over to a corner of the club that had a couch, chairs, and coffee tables.

Gene took her hand in his. "Honey, Allison is not coming tonight. She says there's a family emergency. I need you to sing the song at the end of the show." Gene paused, looking pleadingly into her eyes and then continued, "I know I'm asking a lot. I know you told me you would never sing the song in public, only for me. But I'm asking you, Kelsey, to sing it for me tonight, please."

She looked at Gene and cannot believe what he is asking of her. He can't be serious! She looked at his face and sees that he is. She wanted to lash out at him and tell him that Ally was using him and humiliating her. But she didn't. She knew he's had a tough week preparing for tonight. She looked down at her hands and looked at her engagement ring. Could she do it? For Gene, yes, she could. She sighed.

"Be straight with me," she said, lifting her eyes to his, "is there really a family emergency?"

"No," Gene said, simply. That's all he trusted himself to say. Gene couldn't tell her the truth. Allison wouldn't come and be in the same room with Kelsey. All the phone calls this week were leading up to this. He could see that now. One call she would be up and excited and the next one demanding and angry. Then, this morning she told him she would not do the show with Kelsey. She went off like a lunatic. It hit him like a bullet between the eyes.

"Okay. I'll do it," she said. How could she not do it? A lot people were depending on this show. She tried not to be annoyed.

"Do you want to rehearse?" he asked, squeezing her hand in thanks.

"Danny and I will go into a dressing room," she answered, shaking her hand from his grip. "Okay, if we just use a guitar?" She stood up and started walking away from him.

"Sure, anything you want, baby," he answered. She threw him a look, clearly annoyed, that said, "Yeah, right."

* * *

Gene

He deserved that. At this moment, he felt the full depth of Kelsey's contempt for Allison and himself. He knew she was doing it for him. He vowed to make it up to her. He was madder at himself for not seeing the situation with Allison for what it was.

* * *

Kelsey

She was so angry with Gene. And wanted to be angrier! But just couldn't. She understood the pressure he was under. They would certainly have a lot to talk about tomorrow. She believed that you teach people how to treat you. Well, Gene was going to have a lesson tomorrow! On her way to find Danny, she stumbled a little. What was that? She felt a little light-headed. Okay, slow down, breathe...

Danny noticed and came over to her. "Are you all right?"

"I'm fine," Kelsey said, leaning against him. "We... we... need to rehearse." Danny looked at her questioningly. "Allison's not coming. Gene needs me to sing Persuaded." Danny rolled his eyes, not surprised. He grabbed his guitar.

"You okay with this?" he asked, as they walked to one of the dressing rooms. He knew how she felt about the song.

"Don't have much of a choice, do I?" she answered, opening the door. She stumbled again, feeling light-headed.

"Hey, there," he said, holding her up. "What's going on?"

"Nothing, I'm fine," she answered. "I just need some water."

"Kelsey," Danny said sternly, looking at her, knowing it was probably more. "Did you eat anything today?"

"It's almost over, Danny," she pleaded. "Just help me get through it, okay?" Danny sighed, knowing he would. He would do anything for her.

"I will if you eat this." he said, opening a protein bar and handing it to her. Kelsey always made sure the dressing rooms were stocked with healthy snacks and bottles of water.

"Okay, okay," she said, taking a bite.

The show went off without a hitch. It was a very relaxed and casual atmosphere. In between songs, Gene and Kelsey answered questions from the various radio stations, magazines, newspapers and spoke about their relationship, minus James. Emily had given permission to talk about her being Gene's daughter. Gene smiled and winked at Kelsey during their songs together. Kelsey responded the way she was expected to, but inside she was angry at him. One of the songs she wrote was called God Help My Man If He's Fooling Around. Kelsey played it up for the audience, shaking her finger at Gene, grabbing him by the collar, stuff like that. It was a way to work out her frustration at him. He played along, but he knew her too well. Gene knew he was in the dog house.

Kelsey felt she was doing a good job of holding it together. There were a few small moments when she felt a little light-headed, but nothing serious. The guys in the band spoke about how they started out in her dad's garage with her brothers. As promised, Dr. Melendez was sitting at one of the tables down front. Kelsey made a big fuss over him by singing a song to him. She also sang a duet with Danny. Finally it was time for Persuaded.

Gene introduced her. "Some of you may know this next song. It's number one on the Blue Grass Charts and just broke into the country charts." Gene paused. "Allison Franks was scheduled to be here to sing it but unfortunately, had a family emergency this after-noon and is not able to make it tonight."

The entire audience groaned. Gene continued. "But not to fear! We have the songwriter here and she's going to sing it for us. She's also a close, personal friend." (*Laughter from the audience.*) "You've been loving her all night. Put your hands together for Kelsey McCoury." The club erupted with applause.

Kelsey stepped out on the stage to acknowledge the applause. Everything started getting fuzzy. What was wrong with her eyes? Her breathing felt funny too. Okay, here we go. "I could be persua— Danny!" Kelsey said, grabbing for him. Then she fainted and hit the floor.

CHAPTER TWENTY-EIGHT

Danny reached her first. Dr. Melendez was not far behind. "Kelsey! Kelsey!" Danny shouted at her, lifting her unconscious body into a sitting position, supporting her head. Dr. Melendez opened his bag for some smelling salts, muttering, "I knew this would happen, damn it." He waved them under her nose.

Gene was right behind him. "Baby, are you all right? Oh my god! What do you mean, you knew this would happen, Doc?" Gene said frantically.

Kelsey started coughing as she became conscious again. "What... What...what happened? Oh, my head." Kelsey looked around at all the faces around her. A small knot was forming on her forehead. Dr. Melendez put an ice pack in Danny's hand with instructions to hold it on the bump.

"You fainted," Danny said. "I told you something was wrong!"

"Okay, show's over," Dr. Melendez said, taking charge of his patient. "Let's move her over to the couch." Gene and Danny each put an arm around her waist and slowly helped her off the stage. The audience applauded.

"Oh god," she said, "I'm so embarrassed."

"I'll make an announcement and get everybody out of here," Danny said to Gene, handing her over to him.

"Thanks, man," Gene answered. Cody was waiting at the edge of the stage.

Kelsey stumbled and fell right into Cody's arms. "I got you, sweetie." Cody picked her up and placed her gently on the couch.

"Thanks for coming, everyone," Danny said into the microphone.

"What's going on, Dan?"

"Is she all right?"

"What happened?" The press bombarded him with questions.

"Kelsey is fine," Danny answered. "We'll release a statement later. Right now, I need you to respect her privacy and let the doctor work. You can exit through the front doors." They all filed out, talking among themselves.

"Will someone please tell me what's going on?" Gene demanded, looking at Dr. Melendez and Cody.

Adam looked at Kelsey. "Okay?" he asked. Kelsey nodded, resigned. There was no point in keeping it from him now. Dr. Melendez explained to Gene about Kelsey's visit to his office that afternoon and his conclusion that she had walking pneumonia and was also very dehydrated. Both Danny and Cody had guilty looks on their faces.

"You all kept this from me?" Gene said, looking at Cody and Danny. He was clearly angry.

"Don't be angry at them, baby," Kelsey pleaded. "I made them promise not to tell you. I knew how important this show was to you and Declan and the club." Kelsey leaned back on the couch. "Could you yell at me tomorrow? My head really hurts." She blinked back tears.

Gene's anger melted away as he looked at her. She was very pale and had a big red bump on her head "Okay." Gene sighed. "What's the plan, Doc?"

"Well, I would like to admit her to the hospital in case she has a concussion. But at this hour of the night, she probably wouldn't get a head CT or room for several hours," he said. "So, I'm going to order IV fluids and administer them in your hotel room. I'll keep an eye on her tonight and in the morning, we'll head over to the hospital for the tests." Dr. Melendez took out his phone and punched in the number of his favorite all night pharmacy for the things he would need.

"Okay, sounds good," Gene said. "We need to find a ride back to the hotel." He looked around.

"Mr. Miller?" Collin, the staff member from the hotel who had taken care of Kelsey that afternoon, interrupted. "I took the liberty of ordering an Uber. It should be here momentarily."

"Collin, I'm so sorry, I know your mother was looking forward to meeting the band and getting her picture with them," Kelsey said, holding her hand out to him.

"Mrs. McCoury don't even worry about that," Collin replied, taking her hand. "You just take care of yourself. My mother will understand.

"Thanks, Collin," Gene said, clearly relieved. That boy would be getting a big tip when they went home.

Back at the hotel, Adam set up the IV and Collin got the bed ready. Gene was in the bathroom with Kelsey, helping her change into her pajamas. Gene gently lifted Kelsey's arms up, one at a time to put her top on.

"I'm sorry, Gene," she said, hanging her head, "I ruined a wonderful night for you."

"Are you kidding me? You didn't ruin anything. The show was great. I should be apologizing to you," he said, taking her in his arms. "I'm sorry you felt you couldn't come to me and tell me what was going on." He held her close. "Please don't ever do that again, okay?" He lifted her chin and looked directly into her eyes. "*Nothing*, absolutely *nothing* is more important to me then you." He held her chin and kissed her gently.

"Okay," she said, returning his kiss. "I'm so tired," she sighed, leaning against him. Kelsey felt like her life hadn't stopped since she started seeing Gene.

"I know, baby, I know." he answered, kissing the top of her head. He helped her up. "Let's get you to bed." He really didn't know but Kelsey didn't correct him.

After she was settled in bed, Adam explained that he would be waking her in two hours and asking her a series of questions to check for concussion. Adam took the first shift and insisted that Gene lie down on the couch and get some rest.

While Kelsey slept, Gene checked his phone. He returned messages from Danny and Cody, updating them on Kelsey's condition. He asked Danny to prepare a statement for the press. The next twenty messages were from Allison. He looked over at Kelsey, sleeping peacefully, with the doctor sitting beside her bed. He deleted everyone of Allison's messages without even looking at them. This woman no longer had control over his life. Then he blocked her number. She could call his manager if she needed to talk to him. He'd better call Alan in the morning and warn him. Gene closed his eyes and tried to sleep.

"How's she doing?" Gene asked Adam two hours later.

"Good," he answered. "She's fully hydrated, and I was just about to wake her."

"She's awake," Kelsey said, smiling at them.

"How do you feel?" Adam asked, checking her pulse.

"Much better," she answered, stretching.

"Good." Adam then proceeded to ask her some questions to determine if she had a concussion. He also checked her eyes and listened to her lungs. Gene held her hand the whole time.

"The good news is, I don't think you have a concussion, but I want a head CT just to be absolutely sure." Dr. Melendez said. "The bad news is, your lungs are still crackling. Does your chest hurt when you take a deep breath?"

Kelsey took a deep breath. "A little," she said, holding her chest.

Adam nodded. "I'll order some antibiotics. You know the drill, bed rest, plenty of fluids, Tylenol for any pain or fever."

"We were supposed to go home tomorrow," Kelsey told him.

Dr. Melendez shook his head. "Sorry, you'll be here for three or four more days, at least, then we'll see." He started packing up all the medical supplies. Kelsey sighed.

"What?" he asked.

"Oh, nothing," she answered. She rolled over and sighed again.

"'Oh nothing' is what got you into this mess," he said, smiling, trying to make her feel better. "Now, spill it."

"Yeah, come on, hon," Gene said, rolling her back toward him. "We can't help you if we don't know how you feel."

"It's just…I hate hotels. I mean, they're fine for a few days, but if I'm going to be sick, I'd rather be at home, in my own bed," she said, a little embarrassed. She sighed again.

"Okay, that's a valid concern," Adam said. "I can't do anything about it, but I get it." Kelsey laughed. He succeeded in making her smile. "Do you want me to admit you?" Kelsey shook her head. She had her fill of hospitals back at Christmas the first time she was sick.

"I'll be all right." Kelsey said, resigned.

"I have an idea," Gene said, looking like a light bulb just went on over his head. "Let me make a call. I may have a compromise." Kelsey smiled at him. She loved how he always wanted her to be happy.

Kelsey went back to sleep and Adam left around 5:00 AM with instructions for Gene to bring her to his office at the hospital later that day for some tests. They woke up around 10:00 AM and headed over to the hospital.

While they were running the tests, Gene called Cody. Cody had a beautiful house on the outskirts of Nashville with a lake. Similar to Gene's home in Colorado.

"Hey, Gene," Cody said. "How's everything? How's Kelsey doing?"

"She's good, man," Gene said. "We're at the hospital right now. They're running some tests." Gene paused. "I need a favor, man. It's a big one."

"It's yours, whatever it is," Cody answered. Cody owed him more than one favor for the way he came through for him that last year of Kathy's life.

"The doctor says we'll probably be here at least another four or five days," Gene began. "Kelsey is already going stir-crazy in the hotel room."

"Say no more," Cody said. "Bring her to my house. You guys can stay as long as you like. I've got a few dates coming up, so you'll have the place to yourself for the whole week. My housekeeper will be here to help you."

"Really? Thanks, man," Gene said. "I really appreciate it."

"No problem, I'd do anything for you, man," Cody answered. Gene felt so blessed to have such a good friend. "Did you see the reviews of the show in the press and on social media? They loved you guys!"

"Haven't had a chance yet," Gene answered. "Kelsey thought she ruined everything. That'll cheer her up."

"You guys should consider moving here." Cody continued, "Kelsey should sing at the club more. Attendance would probably double."

"We've been talking about it," Gene said.

"Let me know when you're ready, I know a realtor who could find a needle in a haystack. She'll find you guys a house you will love," Cody said.

"Thanks, man. I will," Gene said. "Thanks again. I'll call you later and let you know when to expect us."

"Hey, Rory Feek was in the audience last night and *loved* God Help My Man." Cody continued. "He thinks it would be perfect for Joey." Joey + Rory were the hottest duo in country music right now.

"Kelsey is going to flip when she hears that! She's a big fan of Joey and Rory." Gene said. "Thanks again, man. I'll call you later."

* * *

Cody

He was so glad Kelsey was better. He had to really fight his feelings to not sweep her away from everyone last night when she fell into his arms. She awakened something in him that he hadn't felt in a long, long time. Wouldn't it be great if she moved to Nashville? Maybe they could do some gigs together. It would be nice to sing with someone again.

After the tests were completed, Gene took Kelsey to lunch in the hospital cafeteria. They had an appointment with Adam at three o'clock to go over the results. He told her about Cody's offer of his house for her to recuperate.

"How nice of him!" Kelsey exclaimed. "Ooh, I'll be the envy of every woman at school when they find out I slept at Cody Rogers house. Too bad he won't be there." She looked off, dreamily, into the distance.

"Hey!" Gene said, pretending to be hurt. "I'll be there, you know."

"Oh, you will? Shoot!" Kelsey pretended to be disappointed, then laughed and kissed him.

CHAPTER TWENTY-NINE

They checked out of the hotel the next day and arrived at Cody's that afternoon. He was there to greet them.

"Welcome, welcome," Cody said as he gave Kelsey a big hug and steered her away from Gene. "I want to say it's worth you being sick so I could have you to my house, but I don't think you'd appreciate that." He smiled down at her as he held her. Kelsey smiled back, losing herself in his eyes. She mentally shook herself back to the present.

"And neither would I," said Gene, pretending to be jealous. He pushed his way in between them. They all had a good laugh. Cody showed them the newspapers and on line reviews of the show. They were all positive and glowing. The future of their production company looked promising.

Cody left for his touring dates the next day. Gene and Kelsey had the house to themselves. Since he and Kelsey were alone, Gene took the opportunity to talk about planning their wedding.

"So, I'm thinking, May," he said as they were finishing dinner that night.

"We have to sing at Nancy's wedding in May, remember?" she reminded him. Gene had been trying to think of a way to thank Nancy for the way she took care of Kelsey back in January. The idea came to him when her parents had invited him and Kelsey to be guests at the wedding. They were going to surprise her at the reception. "Besides, I can't plan a wedding in a month!"

"Oh yeah, right. And isn't it someone's birthday too? Do you remember who?" he asked her innocently. She gave him one of her looks. "Mine!" she told him indignantly.

"Oh right, how could I forget? Okay, how about June?" he asked. "It'll be beautiful by the lake at that time of year. That gives you two months."

"That sounds nice. But let's keep it simple," she said. "Just our kids, my mom, and Danny. Hey, would your Mom come up from Florida?"

"Yes, she would. She's been wanting to reconnect with your mom. This is the perfect opportunity." Gene said.

"Mom would love that!" Kelsey said. "I always felt bad about them losing their friendship because of us."

"What about your brothers and sisters?" Gene asked. They were a sensitive subject since that last meeting at school when she confronted them about everything.

Kelsey stiffened. "We've both done the big wedding thing. I'd like to keep it very small. We can have them over to the house over the summer." Kelsey picked up their plates and started scraping them in the sink before putting them in the dishwasher.

Umm. That didn't sound good. "What about your dad?" Gene asked quietly. "Don't you want him to give you away?" He knew for a fact that she hadn't forgiven him or even talked to him about their relationship.

"No. PJ will give me away," Kelsey answered abruptly. "Dad doesn't know who I am half the time. The other half, he thinks I'm still married to Pete."

"Okay, whatever you want, baby," Gene said quietly. He didn't think she had forgiven any of them. Gene had renewed his friendship with Rob and Jerry since that meeting and they had told him Kelsey was still a little reserved with them. They really wanted things to be the way they were before. Toni told him Kelsey rarely speaks to Sandy. They had all been so close growing up. He needed to think of a way to fix this.

They spent the rest of the evening planning the ceremony at the lake and reception to follow at the house. Kelsey wanted it to be very simple. Rustic country. Emily would be her maid of honor, PJ would give her away, and Sophie would be the flower girl. She would shop for dresses and clothes for Gene when they got home. She would also have to find a caterer and a florist. Emily and Maria would help her. Kelsey hoped she would have enough time. Gene was in charge of the honeymoon.

Waking early the next morning, Gene cuddled next to Kelsey and started kissing her neck. "I thought you were going fishing," she said, half asleep.

"I am," he answered, nuzzling her neck. "In a little while." He rolled her over and kissed her passionately, making love to her. When they were finished, he put his fishing clothes on, kissed her goodbye, and left for the lake.

"Love you," she said, sleepily.

"Love you more," he answered, smiling at her as she rolled over and went back to sleep.

Kelsey planned on taking it easy the whole day. She was still on medication for the pneumonia and not out of the woods yet. She took the opportunity to read the rest of Gene's letters. She spread them out on the bed. Kelsey had been reading a few a week since her mother had given them to her. They were so full of emotion. Sometimes he was mad, sometimes sad. Sometimes they were accusatory, sometimes just full of news from the road. Never happy. They all told her how much he missed her. He seemed to be going through a lot of the same emotions that she was at the same time. He described seeing her from a distance when he was in town. Kelsey wished she had known that. She would have looked for him. She cried for Gene with every letter she read. He had been through his own hell at the hands of her family. Gene had told her of his struggle with alcohol and drugs over the years. She couldn't help but feel guilty about that. Kelsey could forgive them for what they did to her but, not what they did to him.

At lunch time, Gene came in the bed room with a tray. It was loaded down with soup and sandwiches.

"Hungry?" he asked.

"Um, that looks yummy," she answered. "Did you catch anything?" she asked. There was a table and some chairs by the picture window in the bedroom. Gene set up lunch there.

"A few. They were small. I threw them back," he answered. He really just loved the solitude of fishing. It gave him time to think and he's written a few songs out on his lake, casting his rod.

They talked about the fishing, a little about the wedding. The whole time Gene kept glancing at the bed, looking at the letters. With each glance, he grew more apprehensive.

When they were finished with their meal, Kelsey cleared her throat.

"So, I finished reading all of the letters except the last one." Kelsey held up the last envelope. She placed it on the table. It was much thicker than the rest.

Gene stared at the envelope, wishing he could set it on fire just by looking at it. His last letter to her.

"Kels, I really don't want you read that letter," he started. "It's... it's... I was really, *really* mad when I wrote it. I said a lot of hateful things I regret." He stopped and started again, "I had just had a run in with your father that afternoon." Gene could remember it like it was yesterday.

Kelsey moved over to the bed, gathered up the letters, and methodically put them back in the box where she kept them. She motioned for him to sit on the bed with her.

"Did I ever tell you about the last year of Pete's life?" she asked, holding his hand.

Gene shook his head. "I'm sure it was very hard," he said.

"Actually, it was one of the best years of our life together," she said. Gene looked at her, surprised.

"Let me backup," she said. "Pete and I had a good marriage. Typical ups and downs with each other and the kids. But basically, we were very happy. Around the time Em was fourteen and PJ was eleven, he started spending a lot of time with the kids, just the three of them. They went on day trips, camping weekends, things like that. Sometimes it was just him and Em, sometimes just him and PJ, sometimes all three of them."

"Weren't you ever invited along?" he asked.

"No," Kelsey shook her head. "And I didn't think anything of it at the time. I was grateful to have some time to myself. Pete was always in a great mood when he got back and would shower me with a lot of love and attention."

"What about before he left?" Gene asked, curious.

"Ah, that's the interesting part," she said. "About two weeks before one of these outings, he would get very moody with me. He'd start picking fights over little things, the way I cleaned, my cooking, like that. It got to where I couldn't wait for them to leave to have some peace!" She laughed at the memory.

"Then the drinking started." She squeezed his hand. "And the verbal abuse escalated." This time she shuddered at the memory.

Gene turned her to him and asked, "Did he hurt you or the kids? Tell me."

Kelsey looked him right in the eye and assured him, "No. Not physically. And the kids never heard the verbal abuse. He was always careful to start a fight when they weren't home."

Gene relaxed a little. "Good."

"In their eyes, he was Super Dad, Mr. Perfect," she said. Then she paused, "I've never told them any of this." Kelsey squeezed his hand for reassurance. Gene squeezed it back.

"Anyway, this went on for about five years until Em left for college." Kelsey continued, "After she left, he cut back on his drinking, we reconnected and things settled into a routine. He still spent time with PJ."

"You know, Emily told me she and PJ saw me and the band at the Colorado State fair once," Gene told her.

"I didn't know that," Kelsey said, surprised. "They never said a word."

"Why would he not tell you? Or the kids tell you?" Gene asked.

"I don't know." Kelsey moved off the bed and went to look out the window. Kelsey seemed lost in thought. "Did you see or talk to them?"

"No," he answered. "The first I heard was when Emily told me."

"That's weird." Kelsey said and continued staring at the lake. Why would Pete do that, she thought.

"Anyway, once PJ left for college." Kelsey continued, still staring out at the lake, "The drinking and fighting started again." She sighed.

"It got very bad. One day, in the middle of a fight, Pete grabbed me and threw me on the bed." She paused. "It surprised us both." Gene tensed up.

"I got up, grabbed my keys, and left. I drove to my parents' house. I was so upset, I was shaking. My mother sympathized. *My father*, on the other hand, told me it was my fault, I must have done something to make Pete push me. We had a terrible argument. I couldn't believe he was taking Pete's side and the things he was accusing me of. When I went back home a few hours later, Pete was gone. I remember he told me he had a doctor's appointment. I packed a suitcase and waited for him. I was planning on going to Toni's house. I had a whole speech planned." Kelsey paused. "Despite what my father said, I knew that what was happening between Pete and I was not my fault, not my lack of 'wifely duties,' as my father so delicately put it. When Pete walked into the house and saw me sitting there next to my suitcase, he burst into tears.

"'Kelsey,' he said. 'I'm so sorry for everything.' He begged me not to leave him. He then told me what the doctor had told him, he was dying and had a year to live." Gene went over and put his arms around her. "The mood swings were due to a tumor on his brain that had been slowly growing over the years. Drinking had helped ease the pain."

"My god, Kels," Gene said. "How awful." Kelsey leaned against him.

"He never told me about the headaches. I wish he had," she said. "Once I understood what was happening with Pete it was easy to forgive him." Kelsey continued. "There was nothing that could be done, medically, so we spent the last year of his life enjoying each other again. It was like when we were first married. We didn't tell the kids until we had to."

Kelsey picked up the last letter and held it out to him. "What I'm trying to say is, I understand your feelings about my father." She said. "I'm still trying to figure out how to forgive him for what he did to us. I understand how you feel." she said again, putting the letter in his hand, "If you ever want me to read it, it will be your decision."

"Thanks," he said, tears in his eyes. He took the letter and hugged her.

* * *

Gene

He breathed a huge sigh of relief as he hugged Kelsey. Thank God, she wasn't going to read it. The afternoon before he wrote it, he had seen Mr. Kelly in the parking lot of The Guitar Store. This man had been a second father to him, growing up. On that day, Mr. Kelly was not feeling very fatherly. They had exchanged some harsh words. Mr. Kelly really ripped into him and he put all of what he was feeling into that last letter. He had been very hurt by Mr. Kelly's words that day. He was going to burn that letter the first chance he got.

Gene couldn't stop thinking about what Emily had told him about seeing the band at the fair. He suspected Pete had guessed about Emily's parentage and was trying to find a way to deal with it. It's obvious he didn't say anything to Kelsey. Neither did the kids. Why?

Later that night, as they lay in bed, Gene said to her, "I've been thinking about what I told you about Em seeing the band." Gene paused. "Do you think he knew?"

"I don't know," she answered. She had been thinking the same thing. The fact that he took the kids to see the band and they never told her. How he sometimes looked at Emily and then lashed out at her. How they had reconnected after Emily left for school. A lot of circumstantial evidence.

CHAPTER THIRTY

June 2011

The big day was finally here. They were finally getting married! What a crazy ten months it had been! Less than a year ago, Gene had no idea he had a daughter, or that he still loved her mother.

Kelsey got up that morning, a bundle of nerves. She couldn't shake the feeling that she had forgotten something. She went over every detail again. It was a very small wedding, just their kids, Danny, her Mom, and Gene's mom. But it seemed there were just as many details as a large wedding. Like Nancy's wedding last month. It was so beautiful. She and David were so surprised when Gene and Kelsey sang for them during the reception.

They were getting married down by the lake on Gene's property by a Justice of the Peace. The lake represents where they grew up and fell in love.

Gene thought he would be nervous, but he wasn't. It seemed like the next natural step. He loved living with Kelsey. He loved having her on the road with him. Kelsey, on the other hand, was not as enamored with the road as he was. She liked to travel but she loved being home more. She would complain sometimes but she was always packed and ready to go when he needed her to be. They had been to Nashville on Fyrebyrds business a few times and she organized the showcases at the Blue Bird Café. Staying for long periods in Nashville was no fun in a hotel room. Especially after Kelsey got sick the last time. They needed to look for a house there. First things first though, getting married!

* * *

Kelsey

Why was she so nervous? She had been living with Gene for the past few months and knew that marrying him was the right thing, what she wanted. Why was she so nervous? It's silly, but she really wished she could talk to Pete about it. Besides being her husband, Peter McCoury had been her best friend. She really missed him at times like this. They had talked about everything. She decided to pray. "Lord, please send a message to Pete to give me a sign. Something that says he approves." Then she recited the Our Father. Now it was in God's hands.

Later the morning, Gene and Kelsey ate breakfast together. Well, he ate, she picked. "Relax," Gene said, covering her hand with his and giving it a little squeeze. "You've got everything covered. I've never seen a more organized event."

"You're probably right," Kelsey answered squeezing back. "Just feels like I forgot something." Kelsey looked at him. "I love you."

"I love you more," Gene said, kissing her hand.

* * *

Danny

Well, the big day was finally here. He had tried to tell Kelsey in so many different ways over the last ten months how he felt about her but couldn't. He saw the way Gene and Kelsey looked at each other and knew she could never love *him* that deeply. He would settle for being her friend. He had a great surprise for her at the reception. She would love it! It was the least he could do for her. Thanks to her influence he had cleaned up his act, no drugs, no booze…well, maybe a little booze. But he was clean and healthy and that's all that mattered.

The family started arriving for a prewedding lunch. Declan and Karen and their kids, Emily and Conrad, PJ and Meghan, Kelsey's Mom, Evelyn, Gene's Mom, Barbara and best man, Danny. Sophie was so excited about her job as flower girl. Karen said she had been practicing for weeks. Kelsey's father still thinks of Gene as the kid who hurt his daughter so many years ago. Kelsey didn't even tell him they were getting married.

After lunch, everyone scattered to their rooms to get ready. The ceremony was at four o'clock. Gene checked with Danny about the surprise Danny had for Kelsey at the reception. Everything was set! Kelsey still had a nagging thought that she had forgotten something.

* * *

Kelsey

Time to get dressed. She was still a bundle of nerves. She hadn't seen any signs from Pete. She took her dress out of the closet and looked at it. Maybe she shouldn't get married? Maybe the timing wasn't right? Oh god, what should she do?

"Mom, are you all right? You seem really nervous," Emily said, coming over and hugging her.

"I am a little nervous, trying to remember my vows," she lied, patting Emily's hand.

"Just think about Gene and your future. If the last ten months are any indication, you are going to have a very happy marriage," She said, smiling. Emily was so happy her mother was marrying Gene. The little girl inside of her was glad her mom was marrying her dad. Just then, the door to her bedroom opened. Two of Emily's friends, Micaela and Sara, came in. "Hair and makeup are here!" Time to get ready. An hour later, Kelsey and Emily were both ready. Emily went downstairs to check on everyone else.

Kelsey was trying to relax a little before she and Emily had to leave for the lake, when it hit her. She had just remembered what she had forgotten! She started pacing back and forth. She had no transportation to the lake! How could she have forgotten such an important detail!

"Emily, Emily," Kelsey said, when Emily returned from downstairs. "I've got to see Gene. Something's come up. We have no way to get to the lake. I thought of everyone but me!" Kelsey was close to tears. Maybe it wasn't meant to be!

"Mom, Mom, calm down." Emily said. "Everything is fine. You can't see Gene. It's bad luck and besides, he's already up at the lake. He left this envelope for you. I believe it has a solution in it." Emily smiled, in on the surprise. Gene had purposely not reminded Kelsey of this particular detail whenever they went over the wedding plans.

Emily handed Kelsey a beautiful cream-colored envelope with her name in calligraphy across it. Inside was a card with two pictures of them. The first one was their prom picture and the other was of the night they found each other again last August. In each picture there was the same look of love that they had for each other. Kelsey read the note on the card.

My Darling Kelsey, right about now, you are panicking about how you are getting to the lake. Am I right? If you look out your window, you'll see your "chariot" is waiting for you.

Kelsey smiled, stopped reading, walked to the window and pushed the curtain aside. There, in the driveway, was the most beautiful car she had ever seen! A white Rolls Royce fit for a queen! She continued reading.

Pretty, isn't it? I thought you would like it. Kelsey, I have loved you since we were teenagers. You've always been my Princess and I wanted you to feel like that today. Now get in that car and let's get married!

Kelsey smiled and tucked the card in her purse. She was no longer nervous. She looked at Emily and said, "Let's go get married."

In the car, on the way up to the lake, Emily started talking about a dream she had last night. Her dad came to her in the dream. "He told me to tell you something," she said. "What was that, honey?"

Kelsey asked, not really paying attention. She was re-reading Gene's note.

"He told me to tell you 'it's your turn'. Do you know what that means?" Emily asked.

Kelsey paled and looked at Emily. She hadn't told anyone of Pete's last words to her. This must be his way to give his approval! Kelsey smiled at Emily and settled back in the seat for the ride to the lake. "Yes, I know exactly what it means."

Gene stood at the edge of the lake as he watched for the car. All the guests were here. Danny had the ring. Declan was tuning his guitar for the processional song. Kelsey picked out the song, but Declan wouldn't tell him what it was. It was a surprise. Sound system was working. Everything was set. All they needed was the bride.

The car pulled up to the set of steps Gene had built into the slope leading from the road to the lake. They were very rustic and tied together Kelsey's whole theme of a rustic country wedding. Gene looked at Danny and said "Time to get married." Danny nodded.

Kelsey looked at Emily and said. "I'm ready." Emily smiled back. The chauffeur opened the door. PJ's arm appeared to help her out. Kelsey took his arm, stepped out of the car and turned her head up to smile at her son. She saw her husband, Pete, smiling back at her. He said "It's your turn, Kelsey. It's your turn to be happy." She reached out to touch him. "Pete," she whispered, and he was gone.

"Mom? Are you all right? You look funny," PJ said. "It's me. PJ."

"I'm fine, son, just fine," Kelsey said. She took his arm, turned, and smiled at Gene, ready to become his wife.

Gene had a huge smile on his face as he watched Kelsey get out of the car, taking PJ's arm. *Gulp!* All of a sudden, he was nervous. His stomach is doing flip-flops! Then, Kelsey turned and smiled at him. That beautiful smile. His heart did a flip. Everything was going to be alright.

Declan started playing. It's the song he wrote for Kelsey, about their relationship. *Down a Rocky Road.* Emily started down the stairs with Sophie, followed by PJ and Kelsey. Gene meets them halfway. He hugged Sophie, kissed Emily on the cheek, shook PJ's hand and tucked Kelsey's arm in his. They walked the rest of the way together.

When they reached the Justice of the Peace, they stopped.

"Everyone, please have a seat," he said. Kelsey and Gene joined their guests and sat on the two white stools in front of the Justice.

"Instead of vows, Gene and Kelsey have chosen to each tell a story about the moment they knew they were in love with each other. Kelsey? You're first."

Kelsey turned to face her guests. "All of you know the story of how Gene and I met. That was my moment, but there was another one in elementary school. I was in the fourth grade. Gene was in sixth. I had just gotten glasses. I thought I looked beautiful! My parent wouldn't dare let any of my brothers and sisters make fun of me. No, they all said I looked great in glasses. At school the next day all of my girlfriends agreed. But at lunch time I was sitting all by myself on the playground, crying my eyes out. Gene came over to where I was sitting and asked me what was wrong. One of the more popular boys in his class, Billy Wagonblast, had laughed and called me four eyes. Gene got real quiet and looked around the playground. When he saw Billy by the slide, he looked at me and said, "Stay here." Gene had that look in his eyes. I knew Billy was dead meat. I followed Gene and begged him not to hurt Billy, he would just get in trouble. He turned to me and said, 'Sometimes a man has got to do the right thing. 'Hey, Billy! Get over here!' he said. And then he punched him right in the nose! "Don't you ever call her four eyes again!" Then he went straight to the Principal's office and confessed to hitting Billy. He got a week's detention. But so did Billy when the principal found out what he said to me. I knew again that this boy was special." Kelsey turned and smiled at Gene. All the guests chuckled. Declan looked at his Dad and said, "You popped him in the nose?" Gene shrugged.

"If I recall, your mother made me a big batch of her famous chocolate chip cookies," Gene said, looking at Kelsey's mother, who nodded. "And you sat with me every day of that detention."

"Yes, I did. We all ended up becoming good friends," Kelsey said. The Justice turned to Gene. "Can you top that?" Everyone laughed.

"Well," said Gene, "my story takes place a few years later. Kelsey's first day of high school. I hadn't seen her all summer. She'd spent the summer in California with her grandparents. She comes walking to the bus stop that morning. White go-go boots, hot pink mini skirt, pink and green striped top and a pink head band. *And* contact lenses. My heart stopped! She looked at me and said, 'Hi.' I couldn't speak. That was it for me! She was just gorgeous. All the other guys at school seemed to think so too. I wasn't having any of that! By the end of the day, I had found my voice, asked her out for the weekend, the homecoming dance, and junior prom. By the end of the school year I had asked her to marry me." Everyone laughed and clapped.

"You remembered what I wore?" Kelsey said, amazed.

"Of course I remembered." Gene said, tenderly.

"Well," the justice of the peace said, "I think that's my cue. If you would both please stand."

Kelsey and Gene faced each other and repeated the vows they had said to other people in their lives but took on new meaning when they said them to each other.

"I now pronounce you husband and wife," said the Justice. Gene and Kelsey just smiled at each other, not believing that this moment had finally come. "Don't just stand there," he said to Gene, "kiss your bride."

"With pleasure!" said Gene. He kissed her soundly.

* * *

Gene

Finally! They were husband and wife! Kelsey looked so happy! He was going to do everything possible to keep that smile on her face. Danny gave him the signal to stall Kelsey. Keep her at the lake. Her surprise at back at the house was not quite ready. He nodded to Danny. He would receive a text when everything was ready.

* * *

Kelsey

Looking at Gene with a big goofy smile on his face, she couldn't help but smile herself. Her life was a complete 180 from this time last year. But for a chance to be with Gene again, it was totally worth it.

The family all started back to the house for the intimate reception they had planned. "Hey, Kels, let's take some pictures by the lake." Gene whispered to the photographer, "We need to stall." The photographer nodded, in on the secret. He took various candid and posed shots. Finally, Gene felt his phone vibrate. *Come on down!* it said.

The Rolls pulled up to the house. Gene and Kelsey walked up the path, hand in hand, to the backyard where the caterers had set up a tent and would serve dinner. Kelsey looked around the tent thinking it was a little large for their small wedding party. Then she saw them, her brothers and sisters with their spouses! And Gene's bandmates! Kelsey smiled, looking at Gene and he said, "It was Danny's idea! All I did was stall you at the lake." Kelsey walked over to Danny and gave him the biggest hug he had ever had! "Thank you," she whispered in his ear. Then, looking deeply in his eyes, she kissed him on the lips. Danny hugged her again.

Kelsey's relationship with her two older brothers and sister had been strained over the last year. Seeing them here, so happy for her and Gene, she was finally able to forgive them. She understood now that they really didn't have a choice at the time. Their father was the "king of the castle." He made the rules; we followed. They were doing what they were told whether they agreed or not. Kelsey hugged and kissed them all. "I'm so happy you're all here!"

The band was another matter. They had told her they were all "too busy" to attend the reception. Kelsey went over to their tables, smiling and shaking her finger at them. "So, I guess your schedules freed up!" She said as they all laughed, Kevin, Cappy, Stucky and of course Danny.

* * *

Danny

He had watched the ceremony with a smile on his face but with a heavy heart. He loved Kelsey but knew she belonged with Gene. He could never love her the way Gene did. The look on her face when she saw her family at the reception was priceless! And she kissed him! He would remember that kiss for the rest of his life.

Gene went up to one of the microphones. "Thank you all for coming. This day is so very special for Kelsey and I. Frankly, if you had told me a year ago that I would be standing here in front of all of you, married to my high school sweetheart and the love of my life, I'd of said you were crazy! Seriously, I'm sure I speak for Kelsey when I say we are so blessed and thankful to be here with today." Kelsey nodded in agreement.

The caterers proceeded to serve dinner. Good food, good wine, good friends. A perfect night. After everyone was finished, Gene and Kelsey cut the cake and the dancing began. They pressed the band into service for music. Kelsey's brothers and sisters joined in just like the old days. Even Gene and Kelsey sang and played. And Kelsey was finally able to sing Persuaded to Gene.

EPILOGUE

*L*ater on, as the party was winding down, Kelsey sat in a chair, holding a sleeping Sophie. She sighed with contentment. She looked around the room at her family and guests. Everyone was talking and laughing. Gene was on stage with her brothers, playing. Danny and her sister Toni were dancing. Rather closely, too. Now *that* certainly is interesting. Her mother and Gene's mother were talking to Emily.

"Here, let me take her," Karen said. "Time for bed, baby girl."

"Okay, Mommy." Sophie said sleepily, slipping into Karen's arms. "Good night, Grammy K."

Kelsey looked at Karen. "That's what she decided to call you," Karen said, smiling.

Kelsey laughed. "I love it!" She got up and wandered over to Gene's mom and Emily, talking.

"Mom, look at this old picture I found." Emily said. Kelsey looked over Emily's shoulder at the picture that Evelyn was holding. It was a picture of her family and Gene's, circa 1972. Probably one of their many Sunday dinners together. Gene was whispering in Kelsey's ear. Everyone looked very happy.

"Where on earth did you find that?" Kelsey asked. She laughed out loud. Did we really dress like that?

"It was in the envelope Dad gave me before he died. I forgot about it till now," Emily said.

Evelyn held the photo next to Emily's face. "We could be twins!" She laughed.

Kelsey froze while their conversation buzzed around her. Pete had given her the picture? Where had Pete gotten it? Why did he give it to Em? How come she never knew?

Oh my god, he did know, and probably for quite a few years. Kelsey looked around. She had to find Gene.

CPSIA information can be obtained
at www.ICGtesting.com
Printed in the USA
FSHW012357191120